SANDFIRE

CAINE: RAPID FIRE BOOK THREE

ANDREW WARREN
AIDEN L. BAILEY

BLACKWING BOOKS

SANDFIRE

Andrew Warren

Cover design by Onur Aksoy
aksoy.onur@iCloud.com

Please visit:
AndrewWarrenbooks.com

Please Join my Readers Group!

You might get a chance to read the next Thomas Caine thriller for free! You'll also get access to special sales, contests, and new release info...

Please visit
AndrewWarrenbooks.com
for more details.
Thank you.

AUTHOR'S NOTE

The events of *Sandfire* take place before *Devil's Due*, when Thomas Caine is still a paramilitary officer in the CIA's Special Activities Division / Special Operations Group...

CHAPTER ONE

SOUTHERN ALPS, NEW ZEALAND

Thomas Caine sensed death in the cold mountain air.

The tingling hairs on the back of his neck, the quickening pulse behind his temples... Signs he had ignored in the past, and the consequences of doing so had been horrific. Never again. He was learning to trust these instincts. He didn't know who, or why or how. He just knew that death would soon find its mark.

As his senses heightened, Caine reassessed his situation and mentally prepared himself. The trek up the steep mountain had been harder than he expected. The air was thin and his breathing was labored. Snow covered almost everything and its powdery depths slowed his pace. His large backpack felt far heavier than it had this morning. The sun radiated both in the sky and off the white shrouded landscape. It was almost blinding at this elevation, where there were no trees to block its glare.

When he spotted a prefabricated hut up ahead, Caine knew his destination was close, so he picked up the pace. The hut would contain bunks, kitchen facilities, and tables and chairs to lay out maps or play cards. A support service for trekkers and campers in New Zealand's cold but majestic South Island. Caine didn't care about any of that. He cared only that the woman he travelled from one side of the planet to the other to meet in person was present.

Pausing for a few seconds, Caine slid his Glock 17 semi-automatic pistol from his parka pocket. He pulled back on the slide, chambering the first 9mm round. Then he marched forward again. He soon reached the crest of the mountain, where the hut stood. The magnificent view of the rugged, snow-capped Southern Alps stretched out before him, filling the horizon.

He took a moment to gather his breath.

A woman stepped out of the hut. The AR-15 hunting rifle gripped tight in her gloved hands was aimed at the center of Caine's head.

"You came?" she said, sounding surprised. "I wasn't sure you would."

She wore ski pants and a snow jacket over her slim figure. He noticed strands of her hair peaking out from under her cream-colored beanie. They were dyed blonde. She'd invested time in changing her appearance.

"You doubted me, Emily?"

"I did." Her lips curled into a slight grin, but she didn't lower the weapon.

"What happened? Why are you suddenly on the CIA's Capture or Kill list?"

Caine knew Emily Argyle well. A former U.S. Army lieutenant with the Military Intelligence Corps, Argyle had been recruited into the CIA around the same time as Caine. While Caine was accepted into the Special Activities Division's Special Operations Group—commonly known as SAD/SOG—Argyle joined the Directorate of Support, in the logistics and foreign station support group. When Caine was tasked with infiltrating foreign countries to 'neutralize' enemies of the state, Argyle was the agent sent in to support him. On many occasions she had equipped Caine in the field, through dead drops and via intermediaries. She provided him with tools and weapons he would never have been able to source himself. She had covered his back on more occasions than she should have. She had always been reliable and forthright.

Yet for reasons Caine didn't understand, something had gone horribly wrong for her.

Emily Argyle had not answered his question, so he prodded. "Two and a half weeks ago, in Yemen, you vanished. The same day, two hundred thousand U.S. dollars disappeared from the Station House's contingency funds. Last week you show up on an Australian Customs surveillance tape at Perth International Airport. Then you disappear again, only to turn up here in New Zealand's remotest corner, asking for my help. You have to admit... it doesn't look good."

Argyle stared down the sight of her Colt AR-15. Less than a hundred yards separated them. Her weapon was the semi-automatic version of the United States military M16 rifle. If her intention was to shoot him, Caine knew Argyle would not miss at this range.

"You need to drop the weapon if you want to hear my side of the story," she said, a slight quavering in her voice.

Caine wasn't ready to relinquish his pistol just yet. "You wanted to talk. You set up this meeting and now I'm here. Do you want my help or not?"

She hesitated, licked her lips, and blinked rapidly for a few seconds. "It's not that simple, is it Caine?" While her weapon remained raised, her eyes darted left to right, like she was expecting other parties to show.

"What if I holster the weapon?" he offered.

She shook her head. "I don't think so. Throw it away."

Their elevation was far above the snow line. There were no trees this high, nowhere Caine could run for cover. Only snow and the occasional low outcrop of dark, jagged rock. Sensing that Argyle would not be swayed, Caine threw the weapon far into the snow. Mentally he marked where it had fallen. Just in case.

"Good. See, we're getting somewhere."

Caine nodded. His favored SIG Sauer P226 pistol remained out of sight in his right parka pocket. As his instructors had trained him long ago, anticipate what a foe might do in advance. Then prepare for those outcomes. Argyle should have remembered that lesson as well, and checked him for secondary weapons.

"Happy now?"

She nodded but didn't lower the rifle. "You come alone?"

"Do you see any friends?"

Argyle considered Caine's claim, then shook her head. "My own people..." she started, then choked back her words as her voice trailed off.

"What the hell is going on?" He liked Emily Argyle, respected her and trusted her. He was hoping they could work this out, that he could bring her in, and in time she would be forgiven. But the lengths she had gone to cover her tracks, and the missing funds... He had to suspect the worst. "Did you steal the money?"

She nodded. "Couldn't have run if I didn't."

"Start at the beginning." He was sweating now, despite the subzero temperatures. There was nothing like having a gun pointed at his head to get the blood flowing.

"We were all doing it..."

"Doing what?"

"Making money on the side, Caine. Unsanctioned activities. Tell me you haven't done that yourself?"

Caine glared at her, but said nothing.

Emily shot him another brief smile, and sighed. "No, I don't suppose you have. Not that you're any saint. Don't forget, Tom, I was the one who watched over your ass. I know the things you've done."

Caine lowered his voice. "Emily, please. I can't help you if you won't talk to me."

She nodded, perhaps finally sensing that she had no other choice. "We were flying Twin Otter planes in and out of the capital, Sana'a, on a weekly, sometimes daily basis. The planes were fitted with long-range tanks. That allowed us to bring in arms and equipment from bases in Djibouti and Abu Dhabi. But once they dropped their cargo, they were flying out empty."

Caine could see where this was going. "So you and your partners used the space to transport personal manifests. Contraband you could sell for a profit on the side?" He was imagining drugs. Probably khat, which was grown everywhere in Yemen. Something like ninety percent of the local population chewed the plant for its euphoric properties. The leaves were consumed the same way Americans drank coffee.

"Something like that."

"What, exactly?"

She shuddered. "Pharmaceutical drugs. Medicines. Vaccines."

Caine was lost for words. Yemen was suffering through some of the worst humanitarian disasters on the planet. The struggling country contained the largest displaced person camps in the world, and was overrun with diseases like cholera, dengue fever and malaria. It seemed cruel that the organizations tasked with helping the people of Yemen were taking medical drugs out of the country for profit.

Still... While criminal, this was hardly traitorous behavior. Caine sensed there had to be more to her story. "What else was on the plane?"

She shuddered again, scared half to death. "Why does there have to be anything else?"

"Because you wouldn't run for that. You would have begged for forgiveness."

"If I tell you, then they really will hunt me down. Kill me. They'll hunt you too, because you'll know. If I say nothing, they might just be okay with me disappearing forever."

"Who are they?" The anger was rising in Caine's tone. He needed Argyle to understand how serious this was.

Her eyes drifted again, as if she expected assassins to pop up out of nowhere and kill them both. It wasn't an unreasonable fear. The hairs tingling on the back of his neck, the pulsing blood behind his temples... Caine assumed Emily was sensing the same unseen danger he did.

"I called you, Caine, because it was the right thing to do..."

When her voice trailed away to nothing again, Caine gritted his teeth. "Emily, just get it out, now!"

"A Twin Otter went down in the Empty Quarter. You know what the Empty Quarter is, don't you?"

"The Rub' al Khali. The largest continuous sand desert in the world. Encompasses most of the southern third of the Arabian Peninsula."

"That's right. A huge, unbelievably hot and lifeless desert." She licked her lips again. She was shaking. It had been a long time since Caine had seen someone this scared. Fear brought out the worst in people and now he noticed the AR-15 was jittery in her grip. The last thing he wanted was to be shot by mistake because Argyle lost her nerve. "Easy to get lost in. Easy to die in."

Caine grimaced. "What was on the plane?"

"Not what, who. Jarod Forster."

"Who is Jarod Forster?"

"CIA, like us. We're friends. Well, more than that. We were close. But he's dead now."

"I'm sorry to hear that. What did he have that got him killed?"

"Leverage, on a data stick. Intel, that if it got out, would compromise the whole U.S.-Saudi relationship..." Once again, her voice faded away to nothing. It was as if every word she spoke brought her impending demise closer.

"Emily?" Caine had tired of teasing information from the rogue agent. Argyle had contacted him, via an encrypted message less than a day ago. She asked to meet him at this location, at this time, for an opportunity to tell her side of the story. Caine's background research confirmed the CIA wanted her brought in for debriefing. And if that proved too difficult, they wanted her dead.

Caine was her last chance to avoid either fate. Emily should have appreciated she had no other friends left. Cooperating with him was her only option now. "What was on the—"

The wind picked up, buffeting Caine. He struggled to stand upright.

Emily too was shaken by the winds. She could no longer hold her rifle steady. Suddenly she wasn't looking at Caine anymore, but the sky above him. Her eyes grew wide with fear.

It took Caine a few seconds to register the sound of whipping helicopter blades.

He turned fast, pulling the SIG Sauer from his parka. A black twin-engine AgustaWestland AW109 helicopter hovered no more than a hundred yards behind him. Three soldiers in white camouflaged fatigues and armed with M4A1 assault carbines rappelled to the surface. As they disappeared in the snowfields, a fourth soldier inside the helicopter locked his weapon on Caine.

Caine dove behind the closest jutting black rock. Gunfire erupted. Bright muzzle flashes and ear-jarring booms exploded around him, sending puffs of snow into the air.

There was a pause as the weapon was presumably reloaded. Caine prepped to return fire but there was no time. The shooting started up again. With a sinking feeling in his gut, Caine realized he was pinned down, with nowhere to go. The helicopter would soon circle around for a clear shot... Assuming the assailants on the ground didn't reach him first.

"Argyle!" Caine called out. He needed to make a run for it or he was a dead man. "Cover me!"

There was no answer.

Then the hut disintegrated in a gigantic, fiery explosion

CHAPTER TWO

The explosion catapulted Caine through the air and smashed him hard into the snow. Winded, he wheezed for a moment before he could breathe again. His ribs felt broken, but when he touched them they all seemed to be in place. He didn't want to imagine the bruising that would soon spread across his body, but that was the least of his problems.

Dazed, he looked up. Only a lucky fall had saved him, allowing his rocky cover to take the brunt of the explosive force.

Regaining his senses, Caine grabbed his pistol from where it had fallen, then stumbled to his feet. Flaming debris lay scattered and hissing in the snow. Cindered flecks fell from the sky like black snowflakes. Thick dark smoke plumed from the wreckage of the hut.

He scanned the skies for the helicopter, and finally spotted it some distance away. It was wobbling in the air, struggling to regain stability. Smoke trails poured from various punctures in the hull. Caine realized the hut's destruction wasn't caused by the soldiers' ambush.

He searched for Emily Argyle, but she had vanished. Squinting in the harsh sun, he noticed ski tracks heading away from the burning hut.

She must have set explosive charges herself, he thought. Remotely detonated them to cover her escape, knowing a kill team would come for her.

Caine realized he had been wrong about her. She'd remembered her training well.

The helicopter's rotors beat in the distance. The aircraft was still beyond firing range. Caine took a deep breath, and reached inside his backpack. He slid out a pair of Elan Ibex Tactix folding skis, and collapsible poles. Working quickly, he rotated the carbon blades until they snapped into place, then fitted them to his boots. He telescoped out the ski poles, and clambered back onto his feet.

The roar of the helicopter's spinning blades increased in volume... it was approaching his position. Caine looked for the armed men who had rappelled to the surface. He saw no sign of them, but there was no doubt they were closing in.

Caine pushed on his poles and kicked his skis, gathering speed as he headed down the trail. He followed Argyle's tracks as they disappeared down the steep mountainside. She had escaped down the opposite side of the trail he had taken to reach her. If he could catch up, he might still convince her to turn herself in. But first he had to escape the helicopter and its soldiers.

Gunfire chattered around Caine. Snow exploded from the compacted drifts.

He pushed harder, increasing his speed, following the fresh ski tracks in the snow. His body curved into an athletic stance, with his knees and elbows slightly bent, and his body leaning forward into the wind. Soon he was parallel skiing, shifting his weight from one leg to the other as he gathered speed. He must have been doing forty-miles-per-hour or more.

Caine stayed on Emily's trail. He had no idea what lay ahead, but he knew he had to follow, or risk losing her. Sharp cliffs and rocky outcrops leered along either side of the trail. There was only one safe route down the slope, and it was growing steeper and steeper the longer he followed it. Yet he had to trust Emily had already scouted a safe path out of here. That was what he would have done.

When he reached a straight stretch, Caine took the opportunity to look behind.

The three soldiers were also skiing hard after him. They too had planned ahead, and they were gaining.

His fears realized, he squatted closer to the ground and leaned hard into the descent.

Fifty-miles-per-hour.

Suddenly the open stretch disappeared, and he plummeted through the air.

He hadn't seen the cliff in time.

He was falling.

Caine held his breath and tensed, until he realized that was the wrong approach. He had followed Argyle's tracks and she had skied off the same point. There was a snowfield below him. He relaxed his knees, letting his legs absorb the impact as he hit a steep slope ten yards below. He crashed into a snowdrift, barely managing to retain control as he again picked up her trail.

At the last second, he noticed Argyle's tracks veered to the right. So Caine did too.

He churned snow in a fast stop, realizing he was only a few feet away from propelling himself over another sharp cliff. Once he was steady on his feet, he looked down, feeling the vertigo as he did. The next drop was over five-hundred-feet at least, and ended in deadly, jagged rocks. There would be no surviving a fall here.

A sudden whooshing noise caused Caine to turn and look behind him.

One of the pursuers had jumped the same cliff edge Caine had.

He was bearing down fast on Caine, so Caine pushed off with his skis, sliding out of the way.

The foe landed behind Caine, close enough to touch. He stumbled for a second as he struggled to regain his balance.

Caine saw his opportunity. He reached out, grabbing the assailant's assault rifle, and twisted the man in a circle across the snow. The soldier lost his balance, and tumbled over the five-hundred-foot drop. His screams echoed through the cold mountain air as he plunged into oblivion.

With the M4 carbine in his grip, and his ski poles hanging by their wrist cords, Caine spun around and fired towards the cliff. The two remaining pursuers had not jumped the cliff above. They stood perched on the edge, preparing for a clean shot when they thought Caine wasn't watching. They hadn't expected Caine to return fire so rapidly. One took a bullet in the chest and tumbled down the cliff. The other was fast enough to duck back out of sight behind the drifts of snow.

Caine took off again, skiing fast along the top of the cliff. He followed the narrow snowdrift Emily had taken between both the rising and falling cliff faces. She had courage for sure. The route offered little room to twist and turn or to control his speed. One wrong move would end in a high-speed collision into the rock edge on his left, or a long fall to his death on his right.

A thunderous detonation exploded behind him. He felt a concussion wave propel him forward, and he almost lost his balance. Caine dared not look back as he wobbled on his skies. He suspected the explosion was a grenade, most likely launched from an M203 grenade launcher fitted to the M4 of the last pursuer. He glanced down at his own stolen M4, hoping it was similarly armed... No such luck.

To his relief the snowfield soon opened up, and Caine found himself skiing down a steep and wide slope. The open plane of snow afforded him maneuverability, but left him exposed to enemy fire. He spotted Emily about three-hundred yards away, zipping and darting through the snowfields ahead.

Now that control was easier and the threat of a steep fall to his death was behind him, Caine glanced back.

The third assailant was gaining.

The helicopter was flying behind the last soldier, and also closing in. The noise of its whipping rotor blades grew louder with each passing second.

Caine grimaced. As soon as the helicopter reached him he was a dead man.

He pressed down on his skis, forcing himself to stop suddenly while turning sharply to face uphill. He swung his M4 up in an arc from where it had been strapped to his back, and aimed at the third assailant.

The man had not expected Caine's sudden attack, and struggled to slow his speed.

Caine fired a short burst. A cluster of three bullets tore through the man's chest. He tumbled fast, snapping bones as his body flew past Caine. The M4 with the grenade launcher also flew through the air. It soared straight past Caine and landed in the snow, too far away to reach out and snatch it.

The helicopter was closing in. Caine could feel the buffeting wind from its rotors.

The assailant in the cabin was in range now. He opened fire on Caine, using the full automatic setting on his M4. Snow exploded around him in multiple white puffs.

Caine turned and skied fast. He bent close to the ice and scooped up the second M4 as he sped past.

He expected another volley of bullets from the helicopter, but when he looked back, it had flown ahead. The AgustaWestland was ignoring him and chasing down Emily.

She's the priority target, he thought.

Caine had hoped to take out the helicopter with the grenade launcher, but it was too far away for any chance of a clear shot. He slung both M4s over his shoulder and crouched down low. He kicked his skis and pushed with his poles, making himself smaller against the wind. He picked up more speed.

Soon the slope became almost vertical, but he realized he still wouldn't reach Emily in time. She wasn't looking back to see what pursued her... She didn't know the trouble she was in.

He knew if he was going to save her life, he had less than a minute to do so.

He spied a gigantic cornice of snow to his left, a towering white embankment built up on one side of the mountain.

An insane plan formed in his mind.

Caine dug in the edges of his skis to slow down. Then he aimed the grenade launcher and fired. The M433 high-explosive round accelerated from the weapon at two-hundred and fifty-feet per second. It struck the embankment and exploded in a fiery red and orange cloud of destruction.

It took a couple of seconds for Caine to hear the snowbank creak, then shudder. Then the mass of snow began to collapse under its own weight.

Caine's eyes went wide as a thunderous rumbling filled the air. The mass of falling snow had transformed into a gigantic and potentially lethal avalanche.

He turned and skied fast, knowing that his and Emily's only chance of survival was to out-ski the tidal wave of snow. Behind them, hundreds of thousands of tons of ice, snow and rock careened down the mountain.

The slope became even steeper.

Caine spotted the helicopter firing at Emily.

She hadn't been hit yet, but it was only a matter of time.

He crouched low, pushed with his poles and willed himself to go faster with each second. He could hear the avalanche behind him, thundering like an angry storm. The falling snow pounded the mountain with crushing force, and shook the ice fields under his feet.

To his relief, he spotted an alpine forest about a mile ahead. If they could reach that, they might escape both the avalanche and the helicopter.

As he pushed forward, Caine knew he had been reckless, but

he'd had no other choice. He had to scare away the helicopter, otherwise Emily and he would remain easy pickings for the shooter inside.

For some reason Emily had slowed and was shooting back.

The helicopter hovered above, firing down on her in long sweeping bursts.

Had neither of them registered the avalanche?

Suddenly Emily keeled over. Caine gritted his teeth. She was hit.

As he skied closer, Caine lifted one of the M4s into position. Acting on pure instinct, he let loose a burst of full automatic fire at the helicopter. Bullets tore into its fuselage, causing it to twist unexpectedly.

Emily looked up. He was close enough to see the agony in her clenched teeth. He could tell she was grievously wounded.

Then she saw the avalanche tearing down the mountain. The fear in her eyes was sudden and terrifying in itself.

"Ski! Fast!" he yelled as he came close to her. "Head for the trees!"

She nodded, her face ashen with terror, and pushed off.

The helicopter hovered directly above them. The pilot struggled to regain control, dipping and turning the aircraft in erratic motions. The soldier inside had given up trying to shoot them for the moment, as he held on for dear life.

The sky became hazy and white. The noise of the avalanche was so loud Caine couldn't even hear the helicopter.

Soon Caine and Emily were skiing side by side.

The forest was getting closer. If they could just reach it...

A propeller blade lanced through the thin air, piercing the snow like a javelin. Caine pivoted just in time to avoid impaling himself on the jagged, torn metal. He glanced behind and saw the helicopter go down beneath the rumbling wall of snow. Its wrecked chassis was tumbling behind them, tossed around like a scrap of paper in a wind tunnel. Consumed by the snow and ice of the avalanche, it was rolling right at them.

"Move!" Caine shouted, encouraging Emily on.

They were racing fast... sixty, seventy-miles-per-hour.

Caine couldn't help himself and looked back again. The helicopter finally thudded into the ice, crushed into a hunk of mangled metal.

The ground shook like an earthquake. Cracks formed in the ice.

Caine and Emily kept skiing, dodging and ducking between falling boulders of snow and ice. When he could glance her way, he noticed she kept touching her abdomen. He was impressed she had made it this far with what he suspected was a bullet wound. Perhaps more than one.

They skied as fast as they could make themselves go. The noise of tearing, grinding metal reminded Caine that the helicopter wreckage was not far behind. It tumbled after them, chasing them down the mountain.

The trees were only a couple of hundred yards distant now.

The tail of the helicopter spun through the air next to Caine.

Its wreckage was careening down the mountain faster than they were.

He couldn't guess how fast they were skiing, with no reference points and the snow wave building around them. If they tripped at this speed, he knew bones would break and they wouldn't make it.

A hundred yards to safety...

They passed a few isolated trees outside the main forest. One disintegrated as part of the helicopter hull tore through it.

Fifty yards.

Then they were in.

The avalanche caught them.

Caine's skis were torn off his feet. His pole disappeared into the blistering white cloud.

The two M4 Carbines were ripped from their straps, and vanished inside the whirling white hell.

Caine felt like he was swimming, pushing against the wall of snow and ice that was collapsing around him.

The trees slowed the avalanche's flow. Many couldn't withstand the onslaught, and keeled over from the impact. But many more remained standing before the natural blitzkrieg.

Soon all Caine could see was white. All he could hear was the never-ending thunderous roar. He lost his orientation, he couldn't tell up from down.

Then he was shaking his head, spitting snow and ice from his mouth.

He pushed his face upwards, clearing it of the snow that had fallen around him. He had no idea if he'd been knocked unconscious. He felt the uncanny sensation of time passing, without him being aware of it.

The forest was still now, although the skies remained white.

He pulled himself out of the snow bank that had buried him, then checked for broken bones or deep cuts. His body was battered and bruised, but luckily, he'd suffered no serious injuries.

Caine climbed to his feet. Miraculously his backpack had stayed with him, and still held a tent, food, and first aid equipment. Tools that would aid him later, when he marched out of these mountains. But first he had to find Emily Argyle.

He called her name several times.

There was no response.

She had been near him when they hit the forest. He headed uphill to the edge of the timberline, then backtracked down the slope. He found bits and pieces of the disintegrated helicopter's wreckage everywhere. There would be no survivors.

Several hundred yards further down the mountain, he found Emily Argyle.

She laid on her back, panting hard, her eyes losing focus. She was half buried in white powder. Her beanie was gone, and her dyed golden hair cascaded across the snow. Her face was pale, and the snow beneath her abdomen was stained crimson.

Caine raced to her and kneeled down in the snow. He discovered two bullet wounds in her gut. She was bleeding fast. When she tried to speak no words came out.

"It's okay." He pressed his hands against the wound to stem the flow of blood. "You'll be okay."

She laughed, as if she were both amused and disgusted by a thought.

Then her eyes rolled up into the back of her head, and she stopped breathing.

CHAPTER THREE

AL JAWF GOVERNATE, YEMEN

As the vast and empty expanse of sand dunes gradually transformed into the rocky edge of an arid mountain ridge, Safiya Naaji concluded it was time once again to be more cautious with her disguise. Her camel caravan didn't care what she wore or who she appeared to be, of course. But most men across Saudi Arabia and Yemen would be outraged that she wore the robes of a man. Even more sacrilegious, she was pretending to be a man, taking on duties that only men were allowed. But as Safiya had reconciled long ago, she had no other choice.

She had ridden five camels two hundred kilometers across the Rub' al Khali, to the Saudi town of Wadi ad-Dawasir. She had ridden back with only two. The four hundred kilometers round trip through the dry, inhospitable sea of sand had been for a single purpose. Her family was starving. Her husband was inflicted with cholera and his body had wasted away to nothing but skin and bones. If she had not traded three camels for wheat, onions, potatoes, salted lamb and hard Saudi riyals, there would have been no hope for her family's survival.

Every day of her journey, Safiya had dressed in her husband's ankle-length thoob and futa wrap-around skirt. She concealed her long dark hair in a head scarf wrapped around her face. The disguise went as far as painting her jaw, chin and around her lips with charcoal to resemble a beard. She even wrapped cloth tight around her already small breasts, so her female anatomy would not give her away. Her husband's ceremonial Janbiya dagger always hung in its sheath on her belt. She would not have been considered a true Yemeni Bedouin without it. When others spoke to her, she conversed in practiced deep tones.

It had been a terrifying three days spent in Wadi ad-Dawasir. She feared she would be discovered at any moment. If she had, the men would have buried her neck-deep in the sands and stoned her to death.

But her ruse had worked. Her saddlebags were heavy with food. It would be enough to last her husband Tariq, and her two surviving sons, Mohammad and Hussein, six months... if she could keep it hidden from the other families of her tribe. Droughts and the looming war in the east were debilitating everyone. Tribes had become ruthless just to survive. She had been ruthless too, risked the long journey into Saudi Arabia for the riyals, because Yemeni rials were worth almost nothing these days. Who knew when they would need funds to buy their way out of future predicaments.

Soon the sun dipped toward the horizon. Safiya's Bedouin camp was only a few hours distant now. Nightfall was a good time to return home, when the chances of her being seen were minimized.

When she found a well she had used since her childhood, she dropped down a bucket, collected the water, and quenched her thirst. Then she quenched the camels. They would each drink near a hundred liters of the lifeblood of the desert. Safiya had to pull many buckets from the inky black hole.

At sunset, she prepared her prayer mat she had long ago spun and weaved from sheep wool as a child. She faced Ka'bah in Mecca and recited her prayers. She gave thanks to Allah that her ruse had gone unnoticed. She prayed that he would see her family through the turmoil and troubles that lay ahead. Finally, she gave thanks to Allah for his gifts... valuable items recovered from an airplane she had witnessed crash into the desert.

With her prayers complete, Safiya wiped away the traces of charcoal on her face. Then she changed into her veil and traditional Sana'ani curtain-style dress. She shuddered when she thought back to what she had done. Would Allah forsake her for her deception? She hoped he would be merciful, and forgive her for doing what she must to survive.

"Allahu akbar," she whispered. God is great.

When the quarter moon was high in the skies and the stars of the heavens shone clear in the cloudless desert night, Safiya rode into her village. After tethering her two remaining camels, she slipped into her family's tent, held aloft by lightweight plastic poles and long guy ropes.

Her two sons and her husband were asleep on mats. She smelt the aroma of coffee and butter hung in goatskins. Well-worn rugs covered the floors.

She went to her husband. The man was thin and emasculated, still collapsed where she had left him three and a half weeks ago. His eyes fluttered as he roused from his slumber. When Tariq recognized her, his dilated pupils seemed to stare right through her. He had no strength to lift his head or arms to embrace her.

"My wife," he muttered, his voice a coarse whisper. "I thought you were dead?"

"Not dead my love. With Allah's grace I have returned, with food and money."

He closed his eyes and soon was asleep again. She felt his arms. They were as thin as the tent poles. There was no muscle or fat left on him.

"You shame us!" a young voice cried out.

Safiya turned towards the sound. Her eldest son Mohammad had woken, and he glared at her with hate-filled eyes. He was only twelve, but he embraced the anger and the rage of a man twice his size.

"I did what I had to, my beautiful son."

"Do not blaspheme before me. I should have gone to Wadi ad-Dawasir. It is man's work. You are just a weak woman."

Safiya smiled at her handsome son, saddened by his words. Their culture dictated that he was righteous. She had defied the traditions of her people and the will of God. "You are too young, Mohammad."

"I am not."

"You don't know the caravan routes through the Rub' al Khali. We can only carry enough water to reach one well from the last. One mistake and you would have become lost, and then died. That kind of death is not pleasant."

"I know the routes. You have no faith in me Mother."

"You are still a boy, Mohammad. I love you too much to risk losing you."

Tariq stirred, mumbled several words. Safiya went to him and gave him water. He sipped small mouthfuls. Soon he was sleeping again. "He did not recover," she said, stating a fact rather than asking a question. She had, perhaps foolishly, hoped that upon her return Tariq would again be the man she had married. Strong, brave and wise.

He was not.

"There is no medicine," Mohammad exclaimed. "He needs medicine."

"I have money now," Safiya said excitedly. She unhooked the goatskin bag from around her shoulder, and withdrew the riyals she had secured. "We can buy the vaccines he needs."

"There is no-one here who can sell us the medicine we need."

"Then I will travel to Al Abr. I've seen UN trucks in its streets before. I will get the medicine there."

"You will not. That is my role, as the head of this family... until father recovers."

Safiya realized too late that their voices were growing louder. Her younger son, Hussein, now sat upright and rubbed his eyes. The eight-year-old boy looked tired and afraid. He came to his mother and she hugged him tight. "Oh my love, I missed you so. God forgive me for being away too long."

"You're back, Mother?" was all he said as he curled into her embrace.

Mohammad remained stoic. His stares continued to be accusing. "The money will not be enough. Al Qaeda demand more and more for their protection. They will want that money."

"Oh, Mohammad, God favored us." Safiya smiled, realizing in her heart that despite their arguing, she was pleased to see her sons again. She had feared they too might have been infected with cholera, but they had not. "When I was in the heart of the Rub' al Khali, a plane fell out of the skies. It was burning as it did, falling like a comet. It was an American plane. One of the black-skinned Americans walked six kilometers before he died of his wounds. I was too late to help any of them, but I did find these." She opened one of the saddlebags, producing three new American-made assault rifles and six shiny pistols. "These are not cheap Kalashnikov imitations. These are the real thing, American weapons. I will offer these to Al Qaeda for money. I will tell them where the wreckage is in return for our protection."

Mohammad's eyes were drawn to the weapons. Safiya immediately sensed a boy's fascination with the instruments of war. Ownership of a gun like these would make him feel powerful, stronger than he was. She did not like the cold joy in his eyes. She covered the weapons, breaking the spell that had gripped him.

"You are not to touch these. Do you hear me Mohammad?"

He looked at her, dumbfounded.

"There are no bullets anyway," she lied, "so they are useless to you."

Hussein stirred in her lap. "Why would Al Qaeda buy weapons without bullets?" His query was innocent, but Safiya worried why a boy so young would even know to ask such a pertinent question.

She was about to answer when she heard the engines of many vehicles approaching the camp. She quickly covered her face so only her eyes showed and stepped outside to see who these visitors might be. Three black four-wheel drives and three trucks slowed to a stop. Men jumped from the vehicles. They were all armed with military rifles. While they wore the traditional and western garb of Yemeni people, Safiya sensed almost immediately that these were Arabs.

With rapid military precision, the men encircled the camp. One fired a burst of bullets into the sky, lighting up the muzzle of his rifle like a flaming torch. The frightening noise was near-deafening in the tiny camp. Hussein huddled close to her and trembled.

Safiya felt like she couldn't breathe. Were these the rebel Houthis invading from the west? Local Al Qaeda fighters? Or some other rebel group with a political or criminal agenda? She could not know.

"Run, my child," she whispered, but Hussein would not relinquish his grip upon her robes. Mohammad stood frozen next to her. The boy seemed too afraid to do anything, again transfixed by the weapons the men brandished. She heard the noise of running water, only to realize Mohammad had wet himself in his fear.

"Run!" she whispered more harshly. "Mohammad, take Hussein to the caves in the mountains. God willing, I will find you there when I can."

He turned to her, his eyes glazed over and unfocused.

A tall, muscular man entered the village. "Everyone, out of your tents now!" the leader commanded as he strutted amongst his soldiers. "All Bedouin men, in the middle here, now!"

Men and women cautiously stepped from their tents. Their children rubbed their eyes, or huddled low to appear small. Safiya turned and prepared to flee with her children, only to notice more of the soldiers advancing behind them. The camp was already surrounded. These were professional soldiers and there was no escape... They were trapped.

"These two," said one of the men close to her, marching to Safiya and pointing to her children. "These two in the circle with everyone else."

"No!" Safiya stood her ground.

He slapped her hard. Her jaw shuddered and she tasted blood. He kicked several times until she fell prone on the earth. His boot pressed hard down on her head, grinding the left side of her face into the gravelly sand. "Not another word from you, or I will punish you like a whore."

Safiya sobbed but dared not move. "Please, my sons are innocent."

He kicked her in the gut. She cried out her pain. The agony was so intense she could not move, other than to curl into a ball. Then the foot returned to her head, pressing down to pin her.

She watched, helpless as her sons were dragged with the men into a group in the middle of the camp.

"One of you!" yelled the swaggering leader. "One of you saw something in the desert you should not have. Which one of you was it?"

He circled the men and boys. Safiya turned as best as she could to get a better look at him. The man was tall for an Arab, with muscles that made his upper body bulge unnaturally. His head was shaved down to nothing, and his neatly trimmed beard was peppered with grey, though he didn't look to be older than forty. A scar ran around the back of his scalp, no doubt from a war wound that had opened up and peeled back the flesh long ago. It had healed now, but the jagged edges where the skin had mended formed an angry red trail across his head.

"One of you!" he shouted again. "One of you will tell me the truth."

No one spoke. Everyone was terrified.

Safiya knew in her heart she was the 'man' who had seen the terrible incident. The fallen airplane, which no doubt had been shot out of the skies by these people. They were looking for it. She remembered the sand storm that had followed after she had rummaged around the burning wreckage, and found the scattered guns... The plane would now be buried in the endless desert. These men didn't know where it was.

The crack of a pistol shot was loud and unexpected. Everyone in the camp flinched at the same moment, including her. She stared with horror... The soldiers' hulking leader had just put a bullet through the skull of one of the Bedouin men. A fountain of blood spurted from the wound as he fell into the dirt.

"He is but the first," the leader exclaimed. "He will not be the last. One of you. One of you will tell me the truth!"

"Sir," one of the soldiers said as he ran to the leader. He was carrying two saddlebags. He spilled out their contents. Three assault rifles and six pistols fell onto the rocky sand.

Two more soldiers came up behind the first, dragging a limp, thin man between them. They dropped his emaciated form in the dirt before the leader's feet. Safiya gasped.

The man was Tariq Naaji. Her husband.

The leader gave no sign of emotion as he put a bullet through the back of Tariq's head.

Safiya sobbed. Her whole life, and all hopes... everything was stripped from her in that moment. Her sons huddled in the crowd of men. She feared the soldiers would kill them all. No one would be spared.

"One of you," the leader announced again in his booming voice, "is now likely dead. His secret taken with him. But to ensure that no one speaks of what happened today, I am taking your boys with me. Anyone talks to anyone, and I will kill them all."

Safiya wailed between heavy sobs. The soldier with his foot pressed against her head grew tired of her distress. He kicked her again, hard in the head.

Everything went black.

CHAPTER FOUR

Later in the night the convoy of trucks, flanked by the three four-wheel drives, crawled into the Al Qaeda training camp. The dark, mountainous terrain provided cover from casual observation, but it wouldn't protect them from U.S. satellites. Nor would it hide them from the unseen drones prowling the Yemeni skies. If they were identified, or recognized for what they really were, swift death would fall from above, far too fast for them to know what hit them.

But Colonel Sulieman Rashid had no intention of dying. He had plans for a future life, full of opulent comfort. Tonight was just one more step towards achieving that goal.

Rashid was a career military intelligence officer of the Royal Saudi Land Forces. He had learned harsh lessons from his brutal past... If he and his men were not diligent, they risked not only their own lives on the battleground, but also threatened their standing within the Saudi community. If Rashid made even a single mistake on this mission and shamed his leaders, his very life would be forfeit. Many Saudi officers had been executed in the past for embarrassing the Saudi Royal Family, and many more would be in the future. He didn't want to be one of those men, which could well be the case if this meeting failed to deliver what he expected it to.

To ensure nothing went wrong, Rashid had strategized and meticulously executed every step of his plan. This was the agreed rendezvous point, and he had arrived not a minute earlier or later than the stated time. His contact would soon make himself known, so Rashid waited patiently.

As Rashid expected, several Al Qaeda militants emerged from the darkness. The men carried AK-47s and old Russian-made RPG rocket launchers. Their weapons and clanking bandoliers of bullets and shells gave the insurgents a confident swagger. But Rashid knew they were no match for the Steyr AUG and Heckler & Koch G36 assault rifles his men carried. To say nothing of the FN Minimi light machine guns and FGM-148 Javelin man-portable missiles hidden in the trucks. His loyal forces wore civilian garb, because a full display of a Saudi military force inside Yemen could be construed as an act of war. But that wouldn't stop them acting as the soldiers they had trained their whole adult lives to be.

No, Rashid wasn't concerned about Al Qaeda. His concern was being exposed... dealing with a sworn enemy inside a foreign country where he wasn't supposed to be. Al Qaeda lived and breathed to see the downfall of the House of Saud, the omnipotent power that Rashid ultimately reported to. If he was discovered making deals with this enemy, it would cost him his life.

But war created odd alliances. The Houthi rebels advancing from the north were waging a ground war in the streets of Sana'a and other cities in western Yemen. They were a common enemy for both Saudi Arabia and Al Qaeda. Neither side wanted these new upstarts changing the balance of power in this down-trodden country. A decade ago, the bombing of the United States Navy destroyer USS Cole in the port of Aden had galvanized Al Qaeda in Yemen. They did not wish to lose the influence of terror they commanded here. Al Qaeda would work with Rashid willingly, at least for the time being. Their objectives aligned. No other reason joined them together.

Seconds after the Al Qaeda insurgents appeared, Rashid's men disembarked from their vehicles in a display of force. They brandished their sleek, modern weapons, ready to slaughter anyone who might think to threaten them. As an added contingency, Rashid had sent snipers into the surrounding mountains the day before. They remained in position, should their skills in distant assassination be required. Just because the two sides had agreed to a temporary alliance didn't mean Rashid trusted Al Qaeda one bit.

When Rashid felt his men had taken sufficient command of the area, he stepped from his four-wheel drive, standing tall and ramrod straight. The scar on the back of his head pulsed and itched in the heat. Long ago, a Mossad agent had plunged a knife into his skull. The blade had penetrated bone, and then brain tissue. The old wound throbbed.

He ignored it.

A man dressed in a thoob and futa skirt with an AK-47 strapped across his back stepped forward. The lights of the Saudi's trucks lit up the insurgent's face. Rashid saw pockmarks like moon craters, shrapnel wounds, and burns that had healed as an ugly mess on the right side of the man's face.

Rashid knew from his intelligence briefs that this man had once been a bomb maker. He was responsible for many of the improvised explosive devices, known as IEDs, that plagued this country. He wondered if the terrorist had been wounded by his own handiwork? Did this man—who used fear as a weapon—still make his IEDs? Or was he too afraid to do so now?

"As-salamu alaykum," said the man. Peace be upon you.

"As-salamu alaykum," Rashid repeated, not that he cared for the wisdom of the Prophet anymore... not since his near fatal wound had changed him, numbed his very soul. He said the greeting only to appease the man before him. "You are Ahmed Khaldun, Al Qaeda Regional Commander here?"

"I might be."

"I've read your file. I've seen all the photographic records. Do not lie to me."

The man nodded, then bowed as his hands came together in prayer. "Praise be to God for the tasks demanded of me today."

"I do have a task for you," Rashid said without emotion. "In these trucks, I have thirty-eight Bedouin boys."

Khaldun rolled his eyes as his mind calculated why this might be relevant to him.

Rashid recognized the need to explain further. These were not educated men, Khaldun included. They didn't see the bigger picture, beyond some fantasy of destroying the Americans, wiping the Jews from the face of the earth, and creating one pure caliphate across all the lands of Islam. "You need to secure these boys inside your training camp. Don't kill them, or harm them too much. Train and convert them to your faith if you must, but I need them unspoiled. They will serve as leverage over a Bedouin tribe north of here. The risk for me to hold them is too great."

"Which tribe?"

Rashid raised a questioning eyebrow. "Why do you need to know that?"

The scarred man shrugged. He opened his palms and hands wide, suggesting he might believe he was as wise as the holiest Imam. "No reason. But the children will no doubt tell me anyway, after you are gone."

Rashid beckoned for one of his nearby soldiers to approach. "Corporal. Point your weapon at Khaldun. If my hand drops, shoot him."

"Yes sir," barked the soldier, sweat running down his brow.

The Al Qaeda insurgents raised their weapons, ready to retaliate. More Saudis stepped forward, their weapons ready to fire. Faced down by the sheer firepower and unwavering will of Rashid's men, the insurgents backed down.

"Khaldun, my friend," Rashid said, as if no threat had passed between them. "Be aware that I provide you with weapons and funds only because you suit a purpose. I allow you to fight the Houthis for me, because they are a greater enemy to Saudi Arabia than you are. For now, at least. Nothing else keeps you in my favor. Therefore, you will hold these children without question, because I order you to do so. And don't think you can deceive me. I know where all your hideouts are, who your friends are, and more importantly, who your enemies are. I know your biggest fear is the American drones. One word from me and the CIA's Predator drones will be over your camps before you know it. You will be blown back to Allah in a million pieces, your shit mixed with your souls."

Khaldun seemed to shrink into the shape of a smaller, older man. Finally, he understood he was completely at Rashid's mercy, just as Rashid wanted it.

"Good, then we have an understanding." Rashid made another signal with his hand for the Corporal to lower his weapon. Then he signaled to the men in the trucks.

One by one a group of six soldiers lifted the bound and hooded boys, and lined them up for inspection.

Rashid's Sergeant, Khalid al Aziz, his bushy eyebrows as thick as his oily mustache, snapped off a smart salute when the work was complete. "Thirty-seven Bedouin boys, Sir. One died from the head injuries he sustained resisting us earlier."

Rashid nodded. "No matter. Thirty-seven it is."

He watched the terrified boys, quietly sobbing, trembling or wetting themselves, as they were led away into the caves high in the mountains. Despite his warning, Rashid believed most would die. The ordeals they would face under Al Qaeda interrogation and indoctrination would be hellish. Those that did survive would likely become fanatical converts to the cause.

The Bedouins whose lives he had interrupted were cursed. Any hope they had that their sons would be returned was false.

Rashid watched the disappearing boys without a trace of emotion. He had a wife, and a family... two teenage sons and a teenage daughter, in a nice home in Riyadh. He tried to imagine how he would feel if they were held hostage in a similar situation? Rage? Terror? Distraught?

The truth was he would feel none of those emotions.

He would feel nothing.

It was the Jewish agent he had battled in Riyadh four years earlier who had made him what he was. A Mossad cell had been identified operating in the Saudi capital. Rashid had led the raid to apprehend or kill the Israeli agents. Unfortunately, the Mossad agents were more proficient fighters than Rashid had anticipated. Three of his men had been killed and one of the agents had plunged a knife into the back of Rashid's skull, piercing his brain.

He should not have survived.

He should not have recovered.

But he had.

But Rashid awoke with a secret, something he had not told any of his doctors, his Imams, his wife or any of his superiors. After his wound healed, he no longer felt emotions. He was empty inside. He did not experience hate, or love, fear, or happiness. He felt physical pain of course, but he wasn't scared by it. He didn't even feel the power of Almighty Allah anymore, of God watching over him.

He felt nothing.

Upon his recovery he passed all his medical and psychological assessments without a glitch... he knew exactly what his superiors wanted to hear. Soon he was back in the Army he had once loved. Perversely, his lack of emotions made him even better at his job. He could make dispassionate choices in any situation, without worrying about the moral or religious connotations of his actions. A world without emotions soon saw his meteoritic rise through the ranks. But it also deteriorated his relationship with his wife and children. Now he avoided returning home, unless he absolutely had to. He didn't care for anyone, anymore. Not these Bedouin children and not his own.

Only one thing drove him now. Comfort. Life was easier and simpler living in a luxurious mansion in Marrakesh than groveling as a beggar on the grimy streets of Riyadh. His self-assigned mission became money; making lots of it. Wealth was all he needed. Everything else in life was pointless.

The thirty-seven boys vanished into the dark mountains, and the Al Qaeda insurgents faded into the night. Rashid turned and signaled it was time to leave.

The next step in the mission was even more important. The plan to find what was missing had to be executed flawlessly. He had a lost airplane to recover.

And once he found it, the secret it contained had to be destroyed.

CHAPTER FIVE

SYDNEY INTERNATIONAL AIRPORT, NEW SOUTH WALES, AUSTRALIA

Caine sipped a Sapporo beer in a modern bar at Sydney's International Airport. He tried to relax as he watched a Qantas Flight bound for Tokyo announce its final boarding call.

It was nine at night and the airport was bustling with activity. Thousands of bright, multi-colored lights announced departures and arrivals. A poster for the latest Hollywood blockbuster hung next to the lounge where Caine sat. The other patrons in the bar consisted of Chinese tourists, European businessmen, women in power suits, and young backpackers.

An aroma of fatigue and jet-lag wafted off the crowd surrounding him. Airports at night always seemed to Caine to be a shadow-realm of the sleep deprived... packed with people neither fully awake nor dreaming in slumber. Passengers stuck in a kind of limbo, between one destination and another, transiting between their past and their future. Caine was no different.

He took another sip of his Japanese beer and waited for his

contact to show. He had not been told who from the CIA would meet him. He had guessed many possibilities, but he had never suspected it would be her...

"Tom, good to see you." Rebecca Freeling stepped up to his table. She hesitated for a moment, then bent down and kissed him lightly on the lips.

Caine felt reinvigorated at her touch, like he'd been in a coma until now. Suddenly he was wide awake.

Her hand rested on his as she maintained eye contact, and stared into his soul. "How are you holding up?"

"I'm fine," he said. His words sounded harsh to his ears, and she gave him a surprised look. He winced slightly. She didn't deserve that, he knew. Rebecca had done nothing to hurt him. It was he who was quietly withdrawing from her, prepping himself for a long period apart she didn't know was coming.

"I'm sorry, Rebecca. I'm just tired. Emily Argyle was a friend."

Rebecca nodded, and touched her long, fiery red hair to fix where it had fallen across her eyes. She wore a charcoal, two-piece grey pants suit and a white blouse over her tall, slim figure. She looked every bit the part of a corporate jetsetter. In truth she was a rising star in the CIA. As a case officer she had run successful operations in some of the world's most hostile trouble spots. She'd been Caine's handler on many occasions, and like Emily, he had come to rely on her.

But it was more than that...

Unlike Emily, Caine was physically and emotionally attracted to Rebecca, and she felt the same way about him. To Caine's surprise, the mutual and sudden pairing had been lasting. For years now, they had met in airports, military bases and safe houses in every corner of the globe. Their meetings usually began with official CIA business. But they almost always ended with the two of them sleeping together, after each briefing or debriefing.

At first Caine had convinced himself their intimate hook-ups were nothing more than fun. Stress-relief, with no strings attached.

But now he was preparing to disappear into a long-game covert operation in Japan, a mission Rebecca could know nothing about.

He had planned on withdrawing from her completely, silently. Slipping away, letting himself disappear from her life forever. The trouble was, their relationship had become more than just physical attraction. He wasn't ready to let go of her. Not now, perhaps not ever.

He almost wished it hadn't been her who had come to meet him. Almost...

She squeezed his hand. "Where've you been? No one's heard from you in four days."

He nodded, remembering his recent ordeal. "I had to walk out of the mountains. Satellite phone was smashed. I couldn't call for help."

Rebecca nodded, expressing her concern. "You can't just disappear like that, Tom. No one knew you were in New Zealand until you showed up in Queenstown."

He nodded, not sure if she was expressing a Company or personal concern. "Would you like a drink?"

"Shiraz. Thanks."

Caine ordered a red wine for her and another beer for himself.

"So," he asked, taking a deep breath, "what can the CIA's Directorate of Analysis tell me about Argyle? Who were the men sent to kill her?"

"We ran facial recognition on the two corpses you photographed. They were both former Army Rangers turned mercenaries. For the last five years, they operated out of Kabul. We tracked their flights out. They matched with flights for two former US Army Green Berets and a US Army pilot, also previously based in Afghanistan. Kabul to Islamabad, then Mumbai, Sydney, and finally Christchurch. From there they vanished, until they showed up two days later for the mountain assault."

Caine thought for a moment. "Did the five know each other, previously?"

Rebecca shrugged. "We're looking into that. Operationally no.

But in a place like Kabul, I'd say all the American mercenaries in town would know one another. At least know of each other."

"So, someone quickly pulled together a hit team to take out Argyle. Someone well connected, with money to burn. Their weapons would have been difficult to smuggle into a country like New Zealand, and helicopters don't come cheap."

"That's right. Unfortunately, the money trail is a dead end. The account funding their operation was arranged through a Russian bank. Naturally the Russian firewalls are good, and they aren't sharing any information."

"Can't hack them?"

"The NSA is trying. No luck so far."

Caine nodded as he sipped his beer. "What do we know about these covert CIA flights in and out of Sana'a?"

Rebecca beamed.

Caine knew her expressions well... she had information of interest and was keen to share.

"Argyle and Forster were part of a CIA operation called SAND-FIRE. They ran a CIA supply route using DHC-6 Twin Otters. They took off from U.S. Air Bases in Djibouti and Dubai, flew in arms and other tech for the field crews operating in Yemen, as Emily said. But she did lie about one thing. She said the return flights carried no 'sanctioned' cargo. That's not exactly true."

"What kind of cargo are we talking about?"

"Off the books prisoners, persons of interest. Mostly Al Qaeda, Al Shabab, Houthis and other captured insurgent leaders. Some of them were renditioned to deniable black sites in Eastern Europe and other places. Some were just dropped from high altitude into the Empty Quarter, the Red Sea or the Persian Gulf."

Caine looked away and sipped his beer. "That doesn't surprise me. But still, that leaves plenty of room to fly out sizable pharmaceutical manifests if they wanted to. About a ton of vaccines per flight, and if they were doing that every day, that adds up."

"Yes it does," she said. "The flights aren't registered because they have to be completely deniable. But I did look into fuel records and flight times. Taking into account extra tonnage, analysis is they could have only stopped off in a few countries to off-load the drugs. One in particul—"

"Saudi Arabia?"

Her head turned suddenly to stare deep into his eyes. "How did you know?"

"Emily mentioned a data stick on the flight that went down. She said it contained information that could compromise the Saudi's relationship with America."

Rebecca tucked another strand of her long red hair behind her ear. "Of course. You said as much in your report."

"What do you know about the plane that crashed?"

She sipped her wine. "This is where it gets really interesting. We're certain it was shot out of the skies with a surface-to-air missile. That's based on the chatter going on between the Houthi insurgents operating in the region. But we don't think they shot it down."

Caine nodded, remembering the hundreds of briefing reports he had read on Yemen over the years. The Houthis were an armed Islamic religious and political movement originating from Sa'dah in northern Yemen. Predominately Shia, the most recent intel suggested they were backed by the Iranian government. They fought against the Sunni led Yemeni Government, which was supported in turn by Saudi Arabia. A new Cold War between the Arabs and the Persians was brewing inside the war-torn country.

The Houthis were key players in the Yemen revolution, and street battles currently gripped the capital city of Sana'a. While not officially a terrorist group, they were accused of inflicting human rights abuses across the country.

Not that the Yemeni Government was much better, Caine thought.

"So why haven't we found the downed plane?" he asked.

"A sand storm hit shortly after it was shot down. Our satellites and drones have been searching for it since your report, but we've found no sign of the wreckage."

Caine finished his beer. Rebecca sipped the last of her wine.

"So, what now?"

Rebecca bit her lip. "I have some news you might not want to hear."

Caine grimaced. "Tell me anyway."

"I don't know why, Tom, but the CIA Station Head in Yemen wants you to find the missing plane before anyone else does. He asked for you specifically."

Caine was silent for a long moment. A part of him had been keen to follow his investigation through to its bitter end, unmasking whoever was behind Emily Argyle's murder. Now that choice had been taken from him. He had new orders. The hairs on the back of his neck tingled and the pulse behind his temples beat loud again. His first thought was that he was walking into a trap. His second thought was that he should walk into that trap willingly, if he wanted to find Emily's killer.

"Who is the Station Head?"

Rebecca flashed him a mischievous grin. "If we're going to continue debriefing, maybe we should go somewhere more private? Away from prying eyes."

Caine finished his beer. His penetrating emerald stare gazed back at her over the rim of the glass. He smiled.

"What did you have in mind?"

CHAPTER SIX

Caine stepped inside the shower, and watched the running water cascade through Rebecca's long hair. Her back was to him, and his eyes followed the droplets as they trickled down her back then ran along the curve of her thigh. He wrapped his arms around her naked body, and kissed her neck. Her skin tasted warm, clean, and wet. What had it been, eight, ten weeks since they'd last seen each other? He had thought that time might have been their last together. But now, here she was...

She laughed, then turned her head and whispered in his ear. "We can talk now."

Caine nodded. The shower and the background jazz playing in the room would drown out any attempts to monitor their conversation. Since they had begun their affair, they had 'debriefed' this way many times.

Talk first. Lovemaking later.

"The head of the Yemeni Station House is Martin Delbridge," Rebecca said in a breathy voice. "He's a thirty-year veteran with the CIA and highly regarded everywhere. In the Eighties he was in

Colombia, fighting the Medellin Drug Cartel and communist guerillas. In the Nineties he was in Kinshasa during the First and Second Congo Wars. Then, with the rise of Al Qaeda in Yemen, he was transferred to Sana'a. He's been there ever since."

Caine took the soap and washed Rebecca's back. "Does he have a military background?"

"No, but he's CIA paramilitary trained, and proficient in most small arms. He's battle-hardened, fought in dirty wars in all three countries."

"So Delbridge has been stationed in Yemen for more than a decade? That's a long time in a country like that."

"Yes." She turned so he could wash her back easily. "When I looked into this guy, I realized how effective he's been. Under his watch, agent mortality rates dropped and informants became more reliable."

"So why are we talking about him in the shower?"

Rebecca turned, and looked him in the eyes. "Tom, don't underestimate Delbridge. My 'unofficial' digging revealed more interesting details. Despite his successes in the region, most people who've worked with him say Delbridge is out for himself. He'll support you so long as you play by his rules. Cross him and he'll do everything he can to destroy you." She took the soap and lathered his chest. Her touch was gentle and smooth.

"And he asked for me specifically?"

"That's right."

"Do you know why?"

She shook her head. "He'll already know you were unsanctioned when you went to meet Emily Argyle. He'll know that you worked with her in the past. My guess is he wants to keep you close, to see what kind of agent you are." She handed Caine the shampoo, then turned her back on him again as she let the hot water saturate her head. "You know how to wash a woman's hair, don't you Tom?"

He applied a generous handful of shampoo to her scalp and massaged it through her hair. "Is Delbridge a patriot?"

"Of course," she said without hesitation. "It's been said that if stars on the wall at Langley were awarded to living agents, he'd be the first to receive one. In terms of actionable intelligence, Delbridge's reports contain far more value than any other asset we have operating in the area. It's probably the reason he's been there so long."

Caine nodded as he worked the shampoo down the full length of Rebecca's hair.

She moaned appreciatively. "That feels nice."

He nuzzled her neck but his mind was elsewhere. He was wondering why Emily had run to Australia, then New Zealand. As far as Caine knew, she had never been to either country. Most agents who ran hid in countries they had worked in previously. They relied on the contacts they had developed and leveraged over the years. Then again, maybe that was part of her plan. Hiding out in an unvisited country would go a long way towards throwing the CIA off her trail.

He still had the nagging feeling that he was walking into a trap. That didn't mean he would fight the reassignment. He would go willingly to Yemen, but with his eyes wide open. Emily might have been a criminal, but she wasn't a traitor. He would prove that she was innocent of that, at least. He owed her that much.

"What do you know about Jarod Forster?" he asked.

"He's a CIA logistics officer like Argyle. IT background, knows how to hack systems. That's how he kept the Twin Otter flight paths off any official records. Digital records anyway." Caine finished washing her hair. She then applied conditioner, raising her arms high and stretching out the length of her full, slim body. She turned to face him again. "Argyle and Forster were an item, had been for several years. From what I've been told, the two were in love."

Caine wondered how many intimate showers those two had shared. Did they use their fleeting intimate moments to discuss the highest secrets of the American Government, as he and Rebecca were now?

"Anyone else on the flight?"

"Yes, the pilot. Charles Li. I've checked out his records, but nothing about him stands out."

"Delbridge was sanctioning the flights?"

"Yes, but not the illegal pharmaceuticals. At least we don't think so."

"Would Emily have normally been on the flight?"

"From what I can work out she should have been. So why wasn't she?"

Caine already knew the answer to that one. "Forster saw something he wasn't supposed to. Whatever it was, he downloaded it onto that data stick as insurance. But whoever that information affected, they knew Forster had it. They decided to shoot him down in the desert, bury the secret again, instead of negotiating with him. I'm guessing Forster knew he wasn't going to make it, so he insisted Emily didn't get on that flight. She didn't. So they went after her in New Zealand."

Rebecca rinsed the conditioner from her hair. Caine finished washing his taut, muscular body. They were running out of excuses to wash each other.

"Rebecca, Emily told me that whatever was on the data stick would compromise the U.S.-Saudi relationship—"

"I know, it was in your report."

They held each other close for a long moment as the water washed over them. They started kissing.

"Anything else I need to know?"

She shook her head.

Caine turned off the water. They dried each other then he carried Rebecca to the king size bed. Her arms gripped him around his neck and her legs wrapped around his waist. They had talked enough. They were silent as they made love long into the night.

Later, when Caine was certain Rebecca was in a deep sleep, he dressed and slipped out quietly.

His last image of her was lying naked on the bed. He wondered if she might have been pretending to be asleep. Maybe she didn't want to make their departure anymore awkward than it was, and spared him a last goodbye.

That was the trouble with spies. Neither side ever really knew what the truth was.

CHAPTER SEVEN

MA'RIB GOVERNORATE, YEMEN

The road from Al Abr to Ma'rib was long and dusty. There was nothing to see except gravelly desert, towering sand dunes and the occasional ridge of barren, ragged mountains. Yet despite their isolation, Kimberley Hustwait was glad her UNHCR Jeep had an armed escort. An armored personnel carrier of Yemen's Central Security Organization traveled along with them. Ma'rib was a hot bed of rising Al Qaeda insurgency. There was no doubt in her mind that several attempts would have been made on her and her partner's lives if the APC wasn't there to protect them.

She looked over at her partner, Jean Marchand. His wiry, weathered frame sat behind the wheel, steering the Jeep over the equally weathered terrain. John Lennon-style sunglasses perched on his face, along with an expression of sophistication that only the French could pull off. Jean firmly believed he was a ladies' man. He boasted that his French accent could get him into the knickers of any young lady he desired. He had put his signature moves on Kimberley when she first arrived in Yemen two years earlier. He soon learned that

Kimberley liked men who could talk about subjects other than themselves. To his credit, after she turned him down, he had never propositioned her since.

Kimberley figured Jean had slept with a quarter of the foreign women working for the UNHCR... the United Nations High Commissioner for Refugees in Yemen. That probably equated to one conquest every couple of weeks. She didn't know where he got his energy from.

Despite the fact that Kimberley had not slept with him, or perhaps because of it, the two had become good friends. He respected her, and chose her for his fact-finding missioning into the middle of bloody nowhere. The Houthi invaders from the north were already causing mass displacement of refugees across the failing country. Jean and Kimberly were scouting out potential locations for displaced people camps. Locations close enough that refugees could reach them without much hardship, but far enough from the conflict to be safe. Access to the limited utilities available in this country was also a consideration. So far, they had found nothing.

"How are you holding up, Kimberly?" Jean asked. His accent was smooth, seductive... She could have almost fallen for him, if she closed her eyes and imagined his words coming from a younger, more attentive Frenchman.

"I don't bloody know," she snapped. Jean would often laugh at her heavy Australian accent. Especially when she slipped crass Aussie slang into her speech, such as lazy 'mad as a cut snake' and 'bloody pervert'. "I wasn't prepared, that's all."

"Nobody is prepared." Keeping one hand on the wheel, he slid a cigarette from a packet of Scorpions in his shirt pocket. He had bought them in bulk during his last trip to Dubai. He placed the cigarette in his mouth and lit up. Kimberley had given up complaining about the dangers of secondhand smoking. Jean would only argue that Yemen's diesel pollution was far worse for her health. 'Would she like the windows wound down and the heat to get in? Or endure the smoothing scent of tobacco in a nicely air-conditioned vehicle?'

Even though he asked this question often, Jean didn't really care what she thought. He knew he was never going to sleep with her. There was no point in being nice.

"How can they do that to people?" she asked. Then she shuddered, as she remembered the scene on the road north out of Al Abr.

About fifty local men, women and children had been gunned down, execution style, on the side of the road,. Their bodies were left to rot and fester in the baking sun. She hadn't expected to see that, not this early in the conflicts. The stench had been horrific. Yet Kimberley and Jean had managed to document it all, taking photos and making notes while the soldiers of the CSO looked over them. Much to her embarrassment, Kimberley had gagged many times. She had seen dead bodies before, even helped clean away the corpses of refugees when they died in camps. But she had never witnessed so many killed in such a brutal and pointless act of violence.

When they got back to Sana'a, an official report would be filed with the UN. She would also send her findings to her contacts in Amnesty International. They might not have stopped this atrocity, but the least she could do was expose it to the world.

Jean waved the cigarette in his hand, circling it in the air to emphasize his point. "These people have nothing. They have experienced floods, droughts and now war. They will kill if it means their own survival."

Kimberley sighed. He was lecturing her again. She knew all this, of course. She'd been working the refugee aid circuit for five years now, through Iraq and now Yemen.

"Have a cigarette, Kimberley," Jean continued. "The smoke covers up the stench of the dead. I know you can still smell them, even now. Scent has the greatest memory recall."

"Jean, you are unbelievable."

He nodded, appreciative of her words. "Oui! I am, aren't I?"

She shook her head. Had he incorrectly translated her dig at him, or had he chosen to take it as a compliment? She could never tell with Jean. He seemed more like an aging rock star than a UN aid worker.

"Why did you decide to do this kind of work, Kimberley? It is not for everyone. There is no shame in saying it is too much, and going home."

Kimberley remembered her previous life back in Sydney. Five years ago, she had been studying economics, politics and Arabic at the University of New South Wales. She surfed on the weekends, and partied with her mates most nights. There had been a string of boyfriends, of course. Impromptu weeks away at raves, beach parties in Bali and Thailand. Upon graduation, she received a position with an international business consulting firm, much to her parents' delight. High powered suits, liquid lunches with the partners... An office cubicle crammed between twenty other graduates on the twenty-second floor of a slick, glass-clad skyscraper. A window over-looking Sydney Harbor, the Harbor Bridge and the Opera House. The view was spectacular. The money was okay. Life wasn't supposed to get any better than this.

But suddenly, she quit. She moved back with her parents to save money. She dumped her boyfriend dejour, a man who loved only his work in share trading. She applied for every job she could with the UNHCR. A month later, her qualifications and language skills earned her a volunteer role in Baghdad. Her parents had almost died of fright when she told them where she was going. They begged her to stay, but there was no talking her out of it. Twenty-four hours later she was inside the Green Zone of Bagdad. Minutes later, she had already witnessed her first suicide bombing.

Life had never been the same since. Work in the Iraqi refugee camps had been hard work. She had been forced to confront and challenge everything she believed about herself. She knew most volunteers didn't last through the first six months, but she was deter-mined. The only thing that got her through her ordeal was the knowl-edge that she was making a difference. Her life was no longer about hedonism, meaningless sex and making gross profits for multinationals. Kimberley had come to realize, until she had come to the Middle East, her life before had been pointless.

"It's not too much Jean. I wouldn't have it any other way. Besides, if I spend one more day in the office trying to work out what the hell happened to those missing vaccine shipments, I'll go mad."

"Trips into the field remind you why you are here? Right?"

She nodded. Jean was good at being sympathetic when it suited him. "I hate the bureaucracy in this country. I've talked to every government department, in length, and no one knows what happens to it. The medicine just... bloody disappears."

Jean nodded sagely and focused again on the road. He took a drag from his Scorpion cigarette.

She gazed through the dusty windshield. They were in the middle of a long strip of the desert, with nothing but sand dunes on either side. This was the edge of the Rub' al Khali desert. The vast sea of sand dunes was greater in size than Jean's home country of France. It stretched all the way north to Riyadh, in Saudi Arabia.

As she continued to stare at the endless stretch of burning sand outside the window, Kimberly narrowed her eyes in surprise. A lone local woman, dressed in a brightly colored Sana'ani cloth, walked along the road ahead. She was at least fifteen kilometers from the nearest settlement. In this heat, it was surprising she had not passed out, or died already from dehydration.

When they drew close to her, Jean didn't seem to be stopping. She was about to ask why he could be so cruel, when the woman stepped out onto the road in front of them.

"Bordel de merde!" he cried out as the cigarette dropped from his mouth. He gave the wheel a sharp turn as he pumped the brakes.

The Jeep went into a spin, skidding through the gravelly sands.

Kimberley tensed, grabbed the dashboard and held on tight. She was waiting for the sickening, squelching crunch she expected when they hit the woman, but... nothing. They jerked to a stop without hitting anything.

"Putain!" Jean yelled when they came to a stop, trying to put out the cigarette as it burned a hole in his frayed cargo pants. "Putain! Putain! Putain!"

Kimberley didn't care for Jean's wellbeing. He wasn't seriously hurt and could look after himself. She leapt out of the Jeep, covering her face with her veil so as not to offend the soldiers of the CSO. She searched for the woman.

She found her standing alone on the road, her head hung and her body slumped. Two of the CSO soldiers had raised their assault rifles at her. They were shouting at her in Arabic, ordering her to get down onto the ground and place her hands behind her head. She wasn't complying. Perhaps she wanted them to shoot her.

"Aintazar daqiqa!" Kimberly yelled back at the soldiers. Wait a minute! Her hands raised, she didn't wait for permission and went to the woman. "Are you okay?" she asked in Arabic. "I can help you? Are you lost?"

The woman looked up at her and stared without focus through her dark, almond shaped eyes. Kimberley guessed she was a Bedouin woman judging by her clothing. She looked to be mid-thirties, probably even pretty behind the veil. There was bruising around her eyes suggesting that she had recently been assaulted. She also looked to be carrying the weight of the world on her shoulders.

"Would you like some water?"

She nodded.

Kimberley took her to the Jeep, calling over her shoulders to the DSO as she did. "We're taking her with us. She needs medical assistance!"

The soldiers grumbled and returned to their APC. They just wanted to go home. It had been a long day, scouting the desert in the crazy heat of forty-plus degrees Celsius. A crazy Bedouin woman was Kimberley's problem now, and not their concern.

Kimberley offered a water bottle. The woman slipped it under her veil and gulped quickly, draining the lot.

"Are you lost?"

She shook her head.

"Is there someone we can take you to? Your family, perhaps?"

"I have no family. They were taken from me, by Al Qaeda." She sobbed, then spoke in articulate and practiced English. Kimberley was shocked that she knew any English words at all.

"I have been forsaken by Allah, for breaking his commandments," the woman moaned. "I saw a plane, an airplane shot out of the sky. An ill omen, a sign of his anger with me. As it fell into the desert, I too have fallen from his grace!"

CHAPTER EIGHT

AL-WATAH BALLISTIC MISSILE BASE, RIYADH REGION, SAUDI ARABIA

Colonel Sulieman Rashid stepped outside into the baking heat and wondered... should he feel annoyed? The burner cellphone in his pocket had vibrated three times. That was a signal. His contact needed to speak to him, urgently. So Rashid paced across the sand, walking far from the administrative building. Moments before the phone had disturbed him, he had been scouring recent satellite images. He was trying to assess if Hezbollah militants were meeting with former members of the FSB near a decommissioned nuclear missile silo in Kazakhstan. He preferred to focus on his work, but he knew if he didn't respond, his contact would keep ringing. He couldn't have that.

"Yes," Rashid said in English, figuring he was less likely to be understood if he were overheard. No one would question that he spoke the American tongue. As a member of the Royal Saudi Land Forces' Military Intelligence division, he was expected to be fluent in many languages. He spoke Persian, Turkish, French and Hebrew just as fluently.

"You're not in the desert. I thought we had agreed?" asked the American. His contact distorted his dialogue with voice changing technology every time they spoke. But Rashid still knew he was an American. In fact, he knew far more about the man than that.

"Where I am is of no concern to you," he answered in a low voice.

"I take it the aircraft is still missing?"

"You worry too much. The sands have buried it. And now, I can no longer convince my superiors it is still worth searching for."

There was a crackling pause. Then the American cleared his throat. "You know if the data stick onboard is found, you and I are effectively done for?"

"It won't be found."

"Don't be so sure. What about those satellite images I sent you? They show a single Bedouin man with two camels, trekking away from the most likely crash site... He might have found the stick in the wreckage."

"Unlikely," Rashid said in a cold, flat voice. "Besides, he is dead now."

"Dead? How do you know?"

"Because I put a bullet in the back of his head."

"Why didn't you tell me?" Despite the modulation, Rashid could sense the agitation in the man's tone. "Well?" the American continued, his voice rising with concern. "Did the Bedouin have the data stick with him or not?"

"No."

"Is there any sign he found the wreckage?"

"No, he had nothing. If he did stumble across the plane, then he had no idea of its importance. And as I said, he's dead now. Any secrets he may have found died with him. His family will not talk. Nor will anyone from his tribe, for that matter. I have seen to it."

"How can you be so sure?"

Rashid wasn't used to other people questioning his operations or his methods. He wondered if he should feel offended about this. "Their sons are being held hostage by the Al Qaeda cell you put me in contact with. If the Bedouin talk, their boys die."

"You didn't just wipe out the whole tribe? Ensure everyone's permanent silence?"

"Such a massacre would draw too much attention, a UN investigation. This way, it is in everyone's best interests to keep quiet."

The American took a deep breath. "That sounds... acceptable."

"For you, perhaps. I don't like that I have to deal with Al Qaeda. The risk to me is high."

Rashid looked around him. The base was built in the middle of a low, rocky desert mountain range. The terrain served to deter civilians from wandering into the area and taking photos. This was a highly secure ballistic missile facility, with weapons aimed at Iran and Israel. Each missile could be loaded with chemical and biological warheads. The base stood ready to take out thousands of enemies with a single strike.

If he was caught with an unregistered cellphone inside this facility, it would be a major breach of security. It could be construed that he was passing classified details to foreign powers. If he were even suspected of such treason, then his life would be forfeit. He had to be cautious.

The American seemed oblivious to his concerns. "So, you're saying you can't return to the desert, to ensure the plane won't be found?"

"You ask too much. Remember my government endorses this operation. They believe it has been concluded satisfactorily."

The American chuckled. "What you should be asking yourself, is what could be on that data stick that could incriminate you personally. This operation might be sanctioned, but neither side, under any circumstances, wants the truth to get out. Imagine what path our respective governments might be forced to take, if that happened? We could be talking an escalation in the conflicts across the Middle East."

"Are you threatening me?"

"No. I'm informing you. Information is power, after all. But before I fill you in on developments here, there's something I need to know. If you needed to, could you mobilize a small force to take out a single target? If the plane is discovered?"

Rashid took a moment to consider the question. He didn't like how the conversation was going. He had a card up his sleeve, as the Americans were fond of saying. He was tempted to play it now, to show this American he did not hold all the power in their relationship.

"Yes, that sounds possible," he said. "But I still feel I am taking more risks than you. Far more."

Another laugh crackled over the phone. "Oh, trust me, I've been busy my friend. I've just got word that the CIA is sending in one of their rising stars, a paramilitary officer in the Special Operations Group. He's been tasked with locating the downed aircraft."

"You want him taken out?"

"On the contrary, I think we should let him be for now. From what I've read of his files, this agent seems highly capable. If anyone can find the plane, he can. And when he does..."

"I bring in my men, destroy him, the aircraft and the data stick in one strike."

"Damn skippy. You've proved again why I have you on my team."

His team? This American made it sound like Rashid was his servant, a dog sent to fetch a bone. He considered how he might have felt in this situation, if the now deceased Mossad agent hadn't carved away his emotions. Frustration? Anger? Rage? Fear even? He didn't know. He could only rely on logic. And the only conclusion he had come to was that he was more exposed in this operation than the American. That wasn't right.

"Who is the agent?" Rashid asked.

"I've posted the name on our shared encrypted website."

"Then hold a minute."

Rashid keyed in the eighteen-digit alpha-numeric darknet

address into his burner phone. The name was hidden in the bogus code spread in volumes across the web page. It was difficult for most people to spot, but Rashid had been looking at this site too many times not to see it immediately. His lips formed the name without making a sound.

Thomas Caine.

He knew nothing about this agent; they had never crossed paths in the past. But it wouldn't take long for him to find out more. He had to admit the American's plan was sound. They would use this CIA asset to do their dirty work for them.

Then, he would be eliminated.

Rashid erased the name and typed in another. Then he cleared his browsing history. It was time to let the American know how serious he was about sharing the risks.

"Does that name mean anything to you?" asked the American.

"No."

"He's flying into Sana'a today. Have your agents wait at Sana'a International Airport. Photograph him. Follow him. Most of all, stay with him. He will lead you to the aircraft."

"You think that I have unlimited resources?"

"You work for one of the richest countries on the planet. Of course I do."

"I don't have access to the budgets your agency does."

"Not my problem. Your princes take too large a cut of your gross domestic product, in my opinion."

Rashid knew he should have been offended by the comment, but he wasn't. That was impossible now. Still, he needed to maintain face, and shift the balance of power. "I will do as you ask. I will reposition my agents in Sana'a."

"Good."

"Before you go, you too should check our website."

Another pause. "Why would I want to do that?"

"I keyed in another name."

"What name?"

"Your name. You see, I know who you are."

The other end of the line went silent. Rashid knew he should have felt pleased, or smug, but his mind was a blank. He instead reflected on how he had come across this information.

Two years ago, on a mission in Istanbul, Rashid had drugged his chief cyber hacker Mansoor Alharbi. He had stripped Alharbi naked, and posed him in compromising positions with a male prostitute. After he regained consciousness, Alharbi remembered nothing of the incident. Or at least he pretended not to.

Weeks later, back in Riyadh, Rashid had visited Alharbi in the middle of the night. He showed the hacker the compromising photographs. He didn't need to explain what happened to gay men in Saudi Arabia. Eighty lashes as a minimum. Or more likely, torture and execution.

Alharbi now provided Rashid with all kinds of illicit information, scraped from the darknet or other illicit sources. Mansoor Alharbi had a wife, three sons and two daughters to worry about. Per Rashid's orders, he had traced the calls on Rashid's burner phone, and identified exactly who he was dealing with inside the CIA.

After a long pause, the American spoke. "All right, you know who I am now. So what?"

"If you betray me, I will send my best assassins after you. You will not live out the month."

"My friend, it doesn't have to be like this."

"No, it doesn't. Pray that we don't have to go down this path."

The American cleared his throat, which sounded odd through the voice distortion technology. "Is there anything else we need to discuss?"

Rashid considered the request. For now, he knew almost everything he needed to know. He would wait until the asset found the aircraft, then send in his soldiers to finish the job. In the meantime, he would direct Alharbi to uncover as much as he could about this man called Caine.

"Just one question?"

"What is that?"

"Everyone on the aircraft thought you were on it. That you died when it was shot down. Since I know you are, in fact, alive, does that mean you are still with the agency? Or are you in hiding?"

The American laughed again. "I'm very much with my agency. Don't you worry about that."

The phone went dead, leaving Rashid to ponder the information he had uncovered... the identity of the man on the other end of the line, and what his ultimate goals might be.

What exactly was Jarod Forster really up to?

CHAPTER NINE

SANA'A, SANA'A GOVERNORATE, YEMEN

Sweat poured off Caine as the sun beat down through the thin high-altitude air. He was starting to believe the CIA was sending him only to very hot or very cold countries. Despite being only a mile above sea level, Sana'a was oppressively hot. The temperature of the stifling air around him was pushing one hundred degrees.

The city itself was a sprawling mess, trapping the heat in its claustrophobic and chaotic maze. Wedged between ragged mountain ranges, its buildings were a mix of old and new architecture, most of it run down. Like many poor cities, Sana'a was crowded and dirty. Thousands of television antennas bristled from the roofs of the clustered buildings. Dozens of shops sold nothing but weapons. Glocks, M16s, AK-47s, shotguns, curved daggers, and every other kind of small arm Caine could think of.

Some streets were blocked by protestors chanting in Arabic. "Death to America! Death is Israel!" Casual commuters slung AK-47s and other rifles from their shoulders as they went about their daily business. Caine sensed nothing would be easy here.

As soon as he had cleared customs, he received a text message from Delbridge. The man wanted to meet at an Indian Restaurant on Baghdad Street for an early lunch. After completing a surveillance detection route, taking an erratic, meandering path to the restaurant to ensure he hadn't been followed, Caine entered the small, dingy cafe. He chose a table towards the back so he had full coverage of the room. His senses were on high alert. He hadn't felt the need to be this diligent with his tradecraft in a long time.

There were only men in the restaurant, and his was the only white face. He was not surprised that everyone else taking in a curry for lunch glanced up at him often. He couldn't help feeling scrutinized. One man in particular, with bushy eyebrows and a mustache, kept making eye contact. Caine stared back at him, and he lowered his gaze. Whoever he was, he went back to drinking his dark, almost black coffee.

Delbridge was calling all the shots, setting this meet in his own turf. Caine didn't like it.

He ordered bottled water, naan and a yogurt dip. As he waited, a Russian made Mil Mi-17 military helicopter shot over the densely packed buildings, only a few hundred feet above the rooftops. He recognized the distinctive sound of the helicopter's rotors.

A minute after the sound faded, he heard and felt the vibrations of a distant explosion.

People stepped outside to see what had happened. Caine followed the crowd outside... to ignore the disruption would seem odd, make him look even more out of place. A thick plume of smoke billowed skyward in the distance.

One of the patrons turned to Caine and muttered in Arabic... He said something about the Arab Spring, that this was another attempt by the Government to destroy a Houthi rebel stronghold. Caine wished his Arabic was better. He had only caught about half the words the man had said.

Soon everyone was back in the restaurant eating again, as if nothing unusual had occurred.

Caine returned with them, and found a fifty-something-year-old Caucasian man sitting at his table. He had parked himself in the very chair Caine had selected, forcing him to take a seat with his back to the room. The man wore a long sleeve grey cotton shirt and light cotton pants. Despite the heat, he wore a jacket over the shirt. Probably to conceal a holstered weapon, Caine thought.

His hair was grey and spiky, and he was putting on weight around his belly. Despite his flagging fitness, his presence was commanding, like he owned this city. Caine recognized him immediately from his file as Martin Delbridge.

"The coffee beans you ordered." Delbridge slipped a paper bag across the table, which Caine snatched up. It was heavier than coffee, and Caine knew the bag concealed a pistol. "Look after that. Direct from Rhine Falls, Switzerland. Difficult to get hold of here."

"Thanks," Caine said. The code phrase meant that the weapon would be a SIG Sauer P226. Rhine Falls was where the company who manufactured the 9mm pistol originated. "This place seems a bit out of the way. Didn't want to meet at the office?"

"Why would I want to do that? I can enjoy an excellent lunch here. You like Indian, Caine?"

"I like all kinds of food, as long as the restaurant's good."

Delbridge laughed, but his eyes looked cold and calculating. "Don't you worry about that now, the food here is excellent. I ordered ahead for us."

Delbridge called over a waiter, and explained that he had pre-ordered a series of meat and vegetarian curry dishes, along with rice and two bottles of soft drink. The waiter hurried off to get their food.

"Never want to stay in one place too long in this country if you can help it," the older man said to Caine. "By the way, you can't drink alcohol here, and the tap water makes you sick. Stick with the bottled stuff or soft drink. Oh—I guess I should say welcome to Sana'a. First time in Yemen?"

Caine nodded. "You already know that it is."

Delbridge chuckled again. The Naan bread arrived. Delbridge

stuffed a piece in his mouth. "Damn skippy. Oh, don't worry about that explosion, or those Yemeni Air Force copters circling the city. They have nothing to do with us. Just the Hashad Tribal Federation. Or Army defectors, or maybe Al-Islah militia. Hell, maybe even the Houthis having words with the Yemeni Army. Someone's always trying to blow someone else to hell out here. I give it a month before one of them seizes control, and we have to move out. Shut down shop, you know? In the meantime, I'll make the most of my favorite restaurants, right?"

Caine glanced around the room. "That's one way of looking at it."

The man laughed again. "You're a funny man, Caine. I did my homework on you. I know everything about you. Even the bits you'd rather forget. Your special forces training and service record. How you were recruited into the CIA's Special Operations Group, the missions you successfully completed. And those that you did not."

Delbridge grabbed another piece of naan from the basket. His movement shifted the basket across the table, surprising a three inch-long scorpion that had settled underneath the warm platter. The insect scuttled across the table, darting between the two men. Caine expected Delbridge to crush it, but instead he let the venomous arachnid crawl onto his hand. He held it close to his face, studying it.

"Careful, Delbridge. I hear the scorpions here can be lethal," Caine said, surprised at the man's bravado.

Delbridge smiled, as he peered at the creature's thick, barbed stinger. "This one certainly is. *Androctonus crassicauda*, the Arabian fat-tailed scorpion. A sting from an adult specimen can kill a man in five minutes flat. They don't bother me, though. You just need to know how to handle them."

Delbridge looked up, and met Caine's stare head on. "Consider this. Anything dangerous, if handled with the appropriate level of care, can be used to your advantage." He dropped the scorpion onto the table then squashed it with his glass. "I have no use for this one." His lips twisted into a smile more suited to a hyena than a man. "Now, where were we?"

Caine took a sip from his soft drink. "You were telling me you know everything about me."

The older man snapped his fingers. "That's right. Like, you and Freeling, for example? That's a wasted opportunity man. You two should really get it together. I mean, a fine looking woman like that doesn't stick around for guys who can't make up their mind."

Caine forced himself to smile. "I hope we can get along, Delbridge. I'm told you can be very particular about the people who work with you. I've heard you like to 'crush' them if they don't live up to your lofty standards."

The rest of the food arrived, and Delbridge twisted his mouth into another manic grin. He waited for the waiter to disappear, then he leaned over the table, moving closer to Caine.

"People can recover from fuck ups and career terminations," he said, all trace of humor gone from his voice. "They can't recover from being shot full of holes, or blown to pieces. You think Iraq and Afghanistan are hell holes? Wait and see what happens here. Yemen is about to disintegrate into a devastating civil war. Hundreds of thousands will die. Millions more will be displaced. It's my job to ensure fanatics like Al Qaeda don't end up with more recruits to their cause, thanks to the mess that gets left behind. I can only achieve that if I have competent people behind me."

Inside, Caine grinned. Delbridge was rattled. Caine had now learned that his contact wasn't the kind of man who liked to be challenged.

"Fair enough," he replied. "So let's get to work. I'm informed you want me to find your missing plane? The one that was supposedly carrying illegal pharmaceuticals out of the country."

"Alleged, Caine. The word you are looking for is 'alleged'. There is no proof there were medicinal drugs on board."

Delbridge dug into his curry. Caine did the same, only now realizing how hungry he was. He still couldn't shake the feeling that everyone in the room was watching them. He hoped none of them spoke English, because his conversation with Delbridge wasn't exactly discrete.

"Why are we here, out in the open?" he asked. "Why aren't we talking in the U.S. Embassy, inside a SCIF where we won't risk being overheard?"

"A Sensitive Compartmented Information Facility?" Delbridge snorted. "Caine, I have more Yemeni spies inside our Embassy than anywhere else in the country. Besides, I preordered at ten restaurants for our meeting. Wanted the NSB to run around tying up resources, trying to cover all the locations," he said.

The NSB, Caine thought. Yemen's intelligence organization, the National Security Bureau. "So that's why the food came out so quickly," he said.

"I use street boys to pass messages, like they did in the Middle Ages. One of the kids on my payroll made the preorder. Means we aren't here long enough for the wackos to send an assassin."

Caine nodded, not sure whether he should be impressed or concerned.

"Caine, let me give you a little perspective. With the missing plane, we're not talking about anything serious here. Three deceased mid-level CIA agents, and a missing aircraft that's already been swallowed up by the Empty Quarter. It's hardly a blip on my radar, not when I'm dealing with a country deteriorating into civil war."

"So, you don't think the data stick on board is a problem?"

He shook his head. "I doubt anything important is on it. But if there is, you have your orders. If you find anything, you destroy it."

Caine nodded, sensing that Delbridge was purposely shifting his emotional responses between one statement and the next. First he seemed angry, then nonchalant. Disinterested then passionate... it was a technique used to throw off interrogators, and he did it well. Caine could get no sense what the man was really thinking or feeling.

Now Delbridge looked impatient. "I only came here to get a sense of who you are. Now I have." He placed his utensils on the table and pushed the food away from him, even though they had both barely started to eat. "It's time to go."

Caine knew better than to ask why they were leaving so suddenly. It could have been for multiple reasons. Most likely, Delbridge had gotten word that they were compromised. All it would have taken was for his phone to vibrate, or one of his undercover bodyguards to give the appropriate hand signal. Delbridge threw money on the table, and they left.

Outside, a black SUV—armored, no doubt—pulled up. What looked to be a U.S. Marine stepped out. He wore casual attire, but was armed with an M4 Carbine, and body armor was strapped over his clothes. He covered the street while Caine and Delbridge climbed into the SUV. Less than five seconds passed before the Marine was back in the vehicle and they were driving away.

Caine glanced behind them. A motorcycle pulled up at the restaurant. A thin man in a red and white football jersey, loose jeans and well-worn sneakers leapt off the bike. He raised an AK-47 and emptied the full clip into the restaurant. Glass shattered. Men screamed and fled. Caine could only presume innocents had just been killed.

The SUV turned the corner, and sped down a narrow street. The driver barely slowed enough to allow a crowd of pedestrians to get out of their way.

"Well, won't be going back there again anytime soon," Delbridge said as he checked messages on his cell phone. He turned to Caine. "Don't worry about it. This is a war zone. Some kid probably thought he could join one of the factions if he could boast he took out two Americans. He'll tell that story anyway, even though he failed."

Caine glared at Delbridge for a second, but said nothing. He opened the coffee bag, withdrew the SIG Sauer P226 and three spare magazines. Working in silence, he checked the gun's mechanisms for wear and tear.

Delbridge smiled again. "Now we go to the Embassy. You can peruse our files, or at least any files you're cleared to look at. We'll equip you with a satellite phone, some local funds, and whatever else you need. Tell you what, I'm feeling generous. I'll give you access to one of my analysts too, to do some leg work for you."

Caine nodded. Delbridge was nothing like he was expecting. It troubled Caine he couldn't get a read on the man. Caine's earlier concerns that he was walking into a trap suddenly seemed even more plausible.

Another Mi-17 helicopter shot overhead, casting a brief shadow on the dirty roads. Instinctively, Caine slammed a magazine into the P226 and pulled back the slide, chambering the first round. He was expecting combat, but when he looked again, the helicopter was already gone.

"You're going to love it here, Caine," Delbridge said, with that same Cheshire grin plastered across his face. "Everyone does, eventually. Or else they go mad."

CHAPTER TEN

Like everything in the country, the U.S. Embassy, and the diplomats and support personnel who staffed it, looked tired and worn. He sensed that everyone was giving up, that they knew they were fighting a losing battle in Yemen. Yet Caine relaxed a bit once he was 'inside the wire', as they called it. With the Marine Security Guard controlling all points of access, at least here he would get some warning if the sovereignty of the United States came under attack.

Delbridge walked Caine directly to the CIA wing of the Embassy, not far from cubicles occupied by DEA and FBI agents. Accessing the restricted area required passing through a series of unmarked doors. Each entry point required a PIN, biometric identifiers, and several other security measures.

Finally, Caine was taken to the Sensitive Compartmented Information Facility. Delbridge left him with a middle-aged, stocky Latino woman who he introduced as Gloria. She appeared surprised when he said her name, but Delbridge didn't stick around to explain himself.

"I take it your name isn't Gloria?" Caine asked when it was just the two of them.

She rolled her eyes. "That's just Delbridge. He says I want to hog all the 'glory' around here."

Caine looked back over his shoulder, then turned to her and smiled. "That his idea of a joke?"

"No one 'round here gets Delbridge's sense of humor." She offered him a seat next to her cubicle. "You must be Thomas Caine. My name is Gabriella Castro."

"You must get hell for that surname."

She grinned. "I do, but not from Delbridge, oddly enough. It's a common enough family name in Puerto Rico where I'm from. I'm just glad they didn't station me in Cuba. Anyway, I hear you're short on time. You're here to find the DHC-6 Twin Otter that disappeared in the Empty Quarter three and a half weeks ago, right? Operation SANDFIRE?"

"That's right."

"Well, lucky you, Thomas. I'm your assigned Intelligence Analyst while you're staying in Spa Sana'a. I suspect we have a lot to cover. You want a coffee before we get started?"

He nodded.

"Just so you know, Black coffee is the only option here. You don't want to drink the local milk. Trust me."

"Black it is then."

Once they were settled with hot coffees in their hands, Gabriella fired up the considerable tools at her disposal. She had internet access, darknet access, and links to all major libraries' online catalogues. She also had back door access into the databases of most intelligence agencies operating in the Middle East, and one into Moscow's FSB. She could request intel from the NSA, FBI, DEA, the Pentagon, satellite imagery from the National Reconnaissance Office... Any of the agencies in the Five Eye's group and several dozen more organizations—some of which Caine had never heard of, were at her fingertips.

But after several hours of data crunching, they had still found no sign of the plane. Each grainy black and white satellite image looked the same as the last; a featureless, barren landscape. The pictures showed only an endless desert, a glowing white oblivion...

The Empty Quarter.

Caine leaned back in his chair, rubbed a film of sweat from his face, and sighed. "Looks like we've exhausted all of your intel sources, and we've found nothing."

She nodded. "A massive sandstorm covered the western half of the Empty Quarter a few hours after the plane went missing. It lasted two days. Wherever that plane went down, it's long gone now."

"No images of it crashing I presume?"

Gabriella gave him a sad smile. "Nada, I'm afraid. No low orbit reconnaissance satellites in range in time. We suspect it was shot down by a SAM because of the gossip in the Al Qaeda and Houthis' chat rooms. But we don't think either faction did the deed. They aren't that sophisticated, and no one is claiming responsibility."

Caine was silent as he contemplated this intel. SAM was a common term for surface to air missile, a sophisticated weapon more likely to be in the hands of Royal Saudi Land Forces than terrorist groups. And the Saudis had motive to destroy whatever secrets Jarod Forster was carrying on that flight...

Gabriella's fingers tapped across her keyboard, interrupting his train of thought. "There's one last thing we could try. The only ones talking about this plane are the fanatics in the chat rooms. Why don't we ask them what they saw?"

Caine frowned. "How do we do that?"

"We boot up Mustang Sally, and off we go."

"Mustang Sally? What's that?"

"You haven't heard of good old Sally? Its new software we're testing. NSA developed it. We use it to hijack an insurgent's online profile, and pretend to be them. We've had some success provoking infighting and manipulating terrorist cells into murdering each other. We made them think one of their own had turned traitor. We have to be careful though. They're starting to suspect enemy infiltrations on their networks. Besides, I'm only authorized to ask questions, not start a riot."

Caine shook his head. "Let's hold off on that for now. What I really need is someone who was in the vicinity when the plane went down. Someone who knows the exact location of the crash site."

She rolled her chair back from her monitor. "Sorry to be the bearer of bad news. No source of SIGINT I have access to will tell you what you want to know. I've exhausted all Signal Intelligence options."

"What about HUMINT - Human Intelligence? Bedouin lead camel caravans through the Empty Quarter all the time. Spot any of them near where the Otter might have gone down? And what about the Saudis? Their military might have been in the region at the time, and it sounds like they had motive to shoot it down."

She shook her head. "The Saudis track our satellites. When they don't want us to know what they're up to, they wait until we're out of range." Gabriella stopped, considered his request, then returned to her monitor. "There might be an option with the Bedouin though. I've mapped all the possible trajectories the Otter might have taken. I can run some algorithms. Pinpoint people or camels in the desert around the time the airplane went down. Then twenty-four hours after the sandstorm abated? But that's still a big area to cover?"

"Still, sounds like our best option so far."

She tapped the keys again. "We'll have to look at each image that gets thrown up individually."

Caine shrugged, and took a sip of his now cold coffee. "I've got time."

For the rest of the day they sifted through the hundreds of images Gabriella's algorithm flagged. Most were shadows that turned out to be nothing... small herds of large desert antelopes known as oryxes, dried grasses, odd rock formations. They found the occasional crashed aircraft or broken-down car wrecks, but the models dated back eighty years or more. They didn't find any signs of the Saudi military, but they did spot lots of tire tracks in the sand.

When they spotted Bedouin caravans, Caine took all those satellite images and studied each one in detail at his own terminal. After sifting through hundreds of photographs, he had still found nothing outside the ordinary. He looked at his watch. It was a little before five in the afternoon, almost the end of the office working day. Jet lag was catching up with him, and sitting around all day was doing nothing to help him remain awake and alert.

"What about this one?" Gabriella called out.

Caine walked over to her monitor. Gabriella zoomed into an image of a single Bedouin rider with two camels. He appeared to be heading south.

"Can you get better resolution?" he asked.

Gabriella ran a program that cleaned the image, sharpened its resolution. The details were still fuzzy, but something about the man bothered Caine.

"Can you zoom in on the face?"

She increased the magnification. The blurry features of the figure's face sharpened and resolved.

Gabriella whistled. "Well I'll be damned…"

The figure they were both looking at was not a man. It was a woman, dressed as a man, riding a camel. Although the image was still pixelated, Caine could tell she was attractive. She had sharp, high cheekbones and smooth skin. He placed her age at mid-thirties. She was hundreds of miles from anywhere. He checked the longitude and latitude. Her location was approximately forty kilometers north of the Saudi-Yemen border. The date stamp was twenty-one days ago.

"What's a woman dressed as a man doing all alone in the desert?" Gabriella asked.

Caine didn't answer. He examined the enhanced image closely, searching for further clues. He pointed to a small black blob, hanging off the camel's side. "What's that, in the saddlebag?"

Gabriella cleaned the image as best she could. The detail improved. "They look like assault rifles."

Caine traced the tiny black line of the weapon's barrel with his finger. "American-made assault rifles. M4A1 assault carbines. At least two of them, maybe more. Are those the weapons Forster and Li would have had on the plane?"

She took a moment to check the records. "Affirmative. Armory records show they were onboard."

"When was this image taken? What time?"

"Twenty-three hours after the storm abated."

Caine thought for a moment. "If she found those rifles at the crash site, then the plane must be within a day's ride from this location. This woman is the only person who might know what really happened out there. Can you run her image through your databases, see if we get an ID?"

"Will do." Gabriella loaded the image into her database, and began scanning records, looking for a match.

Caine returned to his work station. He had a lead, but nothing concrete. Now he needed to refine his research. He focused on word matches, looking for anything that connected a Bedouin woman with American assault rifles, downed aircraft, illegal arms trade and the Empty Quarter. After a dozen search combinations, he noticed one name kept popping up...

Kimberley Hustwait.

He ran a search on her. The best match was an Australian. Twenty-eight. UNHCR aid worker based in Sana'a. In country two years. No criminal record, and she wasn't on any of the foreign agent or terrorism databases.

Caine studied her photographs, sourced from her Facebook, Instagram and LinkedIn profiles. She had long, light brown hair, a tall slim build, hazel eyes and a button nose. She was pretty. Always smiling in her photos, and always surrounded by friends.

He hacked into the UN intranet and found her employee files. Moderate pay package for someone her age, but nothing special. Good performance reviews. A note that she was sometimes a bit 'too eager' to speak her mind. Then he discovered she had recently visited Ma'rib Governorate. That region skirted the Empty Quarter desert...

Can't be a coincidence, he thought.

"Gabriella?" he called over his shoulder.

"Yes, Thomas?"

"I need everything you can find for me on a Kimberly Hustwait. I just forwarded you her Australian Tax File Number. I need to know where we can find her, and as quickly as possible."

"Will do."

It only took a few seconds for Gabriella to get a hit. "Thomas, you won't believe this."

"What?"

"Ms. Hustewait is downstairs. She's scheduled to see one of our Immigration and Customs Enforcement officers, Matthew Quinn. Her interview starts in ten minutes."

CHAPTER ELEVEN

After months of frustration, trying and failing to secure a meeting with the U.S. Immigration and Customs Enforcement agency, Kimberly Hustwait was ready to give up. This had been another long day of waiting, with nothing to show for it. She was just about to leave the building, when she was suddenly ushered inside a secure meeting room.

The room was bare and the walls were off-white. The only furniture was a table and three chairs. An aide instructed her to take a seat, then left her alone. Knowing that she was on American sovereign territory, she removed her headscarf. Here, she could be free of the concealing clothing this country demanded she wear.

Thirty seconds later, a new man entered. Kimberley found herself staring, unable to tear her eyes away from him. She was surprised that someone of his physique worked for such an innocuous agency. The man was tall, lean and very muscular, built like a track and field athlete or a swimmer.

His handsome face and strong jaw line were framed by thick, short brown hair. He looked about thirty... Maybe a little older, but not much. What struck her most about his appearance were his eyes... He had the greenest emerald-like eyes she had ever seen, and now they were locked onto her. His hand reached out to shake hers in a firm grip.

"Matthew Quinn," he said. His American accent sounded West Coast. "I'm from Immigration and Customs Enforcement. How can I help you today, Ms. Hustwait?"

He sat opposite her, relaxed but alert.

Kimberley didn't know what to make of him. She had been a surfer most of her teenage and adult life. She had built up her muscle tone, and now worked hard with weights to maintain it, since there was no surfing in Yemen. This man looked like he followed a similar regime. He was no 'gym rat', but rather a natural athlete, who stayed in shape through the rigors of his day-to-day activities. He looked like someone who worked in the field in some capacity, a man of action. Perhaps even a former soldier.

To Kimberly, he just didn't seem to be the kind of man who interviewed people all day from behind a desk.

"Call me Kimberley, please." She was embarrassed to hear her voice crack a bit.

"What can I do for you, Kimberley?"

"Well—" She froze, and her voice trailed off... She didn't know where to start. She hadn't expected someone here to be this keen to hear her story. She took a deep breath, gathering her courage. "Let me ask you a question, Matthew. Am I talking to the right person? Do you have authority to do something about the pharmaceuticals that go missing from the UNHCR shipments coming into Yemen each week?"

He smiled, and inside she swooned. When he smiled he was even more attractive. She hoped he was a surfer. That would be a good starting point for casual conversation later. Maybe a date, if the opportunity came up and if he didn't turn out to be a jerk.

"You know you're talking to the U.S. Government?" he asked. "We have no authority over Yemen's politics, or its police matters."

She grinned, expecting this response. "Of course, of course,

Matthew. But I have reliable information that someone from your Embassy was checking one of our HCR shipping containers. In the Port of Aden, three months ago."

"You're only bringing this information to us now?"

She laughed, then frowned. It seemed like this Matthew was going to be a jerk after all. "No, I came to you about this three months ago. This is the first time someone senior has taken the time to speak with me. Are you in a senior position, Matthew?"

Kimberley winced, as she realized she was repeating his name a lot. To her embarrassment, she was trying it out. She found herself wishing he wasn't so good looking.

"The authority I command is considerable, yes," he replied.

"That sounds like bureaucratic speak to me."

He laughed, as if he found her sense of humor refreshing. This was not going at all how she planned. "Well, let's see. What information do you have, Kimberley?"

"I have these." She passed over a stack of photographs she had brought with her. They were of an American she had secretly photographed three months ago, inspecting a row of twenty-foot shipping containers. These specific containers held pharmaceuticals for the UNHCR aid program. Vaccines to combat malaria, cholera and other debilitating pandemic infections.

Rather than confronting the man, she decided to gather evidence first. The photographs clearly captured the man offering the port master—or whatever he was called—a thick envelope. No doubt it was heavy with cash.

"You'll notice the container was full when he inspected it." She handed over more photographs. "Now later, when I came to collect the medicines, this is what I found." The next series of photos showed stacks of empty crates.

The man called Matthew examined the pictures. "I'm sorry for your loss, Kimberley. But what makes you believe this man works for our Embassy?"

She grinned again, prepared for this question. She slid more pictures across the table. "Here, we see the same man entering the Embassy in the morning. And here is another photograph of him leaving in the afternoon, on the same day. I have the same photos taken over several months. He works office hours when he's not at the airport, or in Aden."

For a moment Matthew Quinn looked concerned. When he caught her watching him, he masked his emotion and smiled at her again. "Seems strange, doesn't it? Out of curiosity, what do you think is happening here?"

Now this wasn't a question Kimberley was ready for. No one in the Embassy had been interested in her opinion before. She had her suspicions what was transpiring here, but she had no proof.

Revealing suspected illegal activities of the U.S. Government inside their own embassy might land her in hot water. Jean Marchand, and others in the HCR, warned her that she might have stumbled into a covert operation run by the CIA. Or one of the American's other, numerous secret organizations. Revealing what she knew might not fare well for her long-term career prospects. Or her health...

But Kimberley refused to give up. She had joined the United Nations because she wanted to make the world a better place. A safer place, for everyone. If getting to the bottom of missing medicine shipments wasn't doing that, she didn't know what was.

"I think someone in your Embassy is buying the drugs cheap. Flying them out of the country to somewhere like Dubai, where they are selling them for profit. Despicable if you ask me. Hundreds of refugees are dying without these medicines."

"I agree," the man said, examining the new photographs. "If it's true."

She nodded, conceding his point. "That's right, if it is true. But you have to admit, I have enough here for you to be at least a little bit suspicious?"

"Yes, but this is a very serious accusation. You have more information, I take it?"

She leant back in her chair. Matthew Quinn was very good at getting to the crux of the situation. It was both refreshing and alarming.

He raised an inquisitive eyebrow. Those beautiful emerald green eyes wouldn't stop staring at her. "Well?"

"Um... Well, let me put it this way, Matthew." There she was, saying his name again. "I've heard, from a reliable source, that one of your planes went down in the Empty Quarter about a month ago. It was carrying a full load of cholera and malaria vaccines. Exactly what the UN needs to stop a humanitarian crisis from unfolding in this country."

This time he did seem interested in what she was saying. "How would you know about a plane in the desert?"

"Bedouins, Matthew, you know who they are?"

He nodded.

"Well, one of them might be willing to help your investigation—"

"My investigation?"

"Yes. You are going to investigate this, aren't you? One of your planes is missing, after all."

Quinn leant back with a contemplative look in his eyes. "Let's not get ahead of ourselves. Tell me what you know, and I'll look into it."

She took a deep breath, centering herself and calming her nerves. "I have an eyewitness—"

"The Bedouin?"

"Yes, the Bedouin. She saw the plane. She knows where it is. In return for your Embassy's help in getting her family back, she would be willing to provide you with the location of the aircraft." She looked at Matthew, waiting for a response. He was staring back at her, but his mind seemed elsewhere. She couldn't guess as to what he might be thinking. He seemed to be working through a series of steps in his mind.

Her own mind began to race. She was starting to wonder if he was an intelligence agent. What had she stumbled into? Was it something far bigger than she had imagined?

"Where is this Bedouin woman now?" he finally asked.

"Ah," she said quickly, grateful that he'd broken the silence between them. "I'll introduce her, once you and I have worked out a deal."

Matthew Quinn stood, then walked over and shook her hand. The skin on skin contact caused her to shiver. It had been a long time since she had felt a tingle like that at a man's touch. When he pulled back, his hand accidentally brushed her hair. "Thank you for your time, Kimberley. I'll look into this, I promise. I'll be in touch with you when, or if, I find anything. How does that sound?"

"Hey, wait a second, I—"

He rattled off her address, as he guided her towards the exit. "Is that where you live, here in Sana'a?"

"Yes, how did you know that?"

"It was on one of the forms you filled out, on your first visit three months ago. I'm just checking to ensure all our records are up to date."

She frowned. Matthew seemed a bit too efficient for a government bureaucrat.

"They're up to date, but if the Yemeni authorities start giving me a hard time, I'm blaming you, Mr. Matthew Quinn."

He led her to the door and the way out. "Thank you for your time, Ms. Hustwait. We'll be in touch."

CHAPTER TWELVE

Despite his exhaustion, Caine couldn't sleep. The distant shootings and the occasional bomb blast reminded him that Sana'a was a city under siege. Houthi rebels, inspired by the revolution in Egypt, had increased their insurgent activities. Their forces advanced in the south, spurred on by a single goal... to occupy this city.

As he tossed and turned, he thought back to his interview with Kimberley Hustwait. She knew far more than he had expected. Now he was worried that their conversation could have been overheard. Someone with access to money, mercenaries and operational expertise had taken out Emily Argyle, Jarod Forster and Charles Li. This was exactly the kind of thing the CIA did well.

Based on Kimberly's photographs, he was beginning to suspect a criminal smuggling ring was operating inside the CIA. Forster and Argyle must have been part of it. If they had felt threatened, they might have gathered evidence implicating the other parties involved. Insurance, to protect them from future reprisals. But whoever Forster and Argyle were afraid of, their ploy hadn't worked. Their former partners had opted to permanently silence them, rather than face possible blackmail.

The theory sounded plausible, except that Caine hadn't figured out how the Saudis came into this.

An explosion sounded in the distance. He felt the slightest tremor shake the hotel's foundations.

Caine sat upright, giving up on any thought of sleep.

He was fully dressed anyway, including his worn desert boots. A field kit was already packed, and rested within arm's reach should he need to leave quickly. Inside the shoulder bag was a satellite phone, water bottles, and a first aid kit, along with rations and other supplies. He had also stowed more tracking devices, like the one he had placed on Kimberley as she had exited the interview room.

He had an SOG Seal twelve-inch fighting knife strapped in a sheath on his right leg. His SIG P226 lay under his pillow, and resting by the pack was an AK-47 rifle. The pouches in his body armor held a dozen magazines of 7.62×39mm rounds. He had purchased the weapon and ammo from a street vendor on the way back from the Embassy. He had also picked up a headscarf, sunglasses, and a khaki ankle-length thoob, so he could blend in with the locals. He was glad he hadn't shaved in days, giving him the beginnings of a beard like the men in the area wore.

Caine paced back and forth, wondering what he should do with Kimberley Hustwait. He didn't know which option carried more risk; going to her now or meeting her in the morning.

He took a deep breath, and checked the tracking device he had placed in Kimberley's hair. The tracer was so tiny she would likely not notice it. It was secured with a powerful glue that would take many washes to come loose. He had tracked her movements using an app on his satellite phone. After the interview she had returned to her home address, and had remained there all night. Caine figured she was as safe as he was for the time being.

He was tired, and he knew he needed sleep. But the distant explosions, gunfire, helicopters and sirens made that impossible. He understood that the hotel was supposed to be one of the most secure locations in the city. Two entire floors were rented on a permanent basis by the U.S. Government. They were protected by Marines in civilian gear on a twenty-four seven rotation. But they couldn't protect the occupants from every potential threat. And Caine wasn't used to trusting his safety to others.

He was about to work through a series of exercises, when the satellite phone rang.

Caine answered it immediately, but said nothing.

"Caine?" It was Delbridge. He sounded frantic, afraid.

"Delbridge? What's going on?"

"We've been compromised." Caine heard gunshots echoing through the line. "Someone in the CIA is behind this."

"What are you talking about?"

"Someone in our government doesn't want you to find that plane. Are you in the hotel?"

"Yes?"

"Get out, now! A kill team is coming for you. Get out, and meet me at Taiz and Ring Road."

"You're compromised too?"

"Don't worry about me. Just leave! Don't tell anyone what you're doing!"

The line went dead.

Caine felt the hairs on the back of his neck rise and the blood thunder in his temples.

Outside he could hear men arguing in Arabic. He grabbed the AK-47, fitted his body armor, and slung his field pack over his back. Then stalked over to the window. He pulled back the charging handle on the rifle, loading the first round. Then he flipped the safety lever to the fire position. Craning his head, Caine snuck a look between the flimsy curtains. Several men scurried across the roof of a decrepit building across the street. They were no more than two-hundred feet distant.

One was aiming an RPG-29 'Vampire' rocket launcher, lining up the sites with Caine's window.

Without conscious thought, Caine squeezed the trigger and

unloaded the full magazine. Thirty rounds of high-speed bullets lit up the muzzle of his AK. His barrage painted his attacker red, as meaty wounds exploded all over the man's body.

But before his target fell dead, the man's fingers gripped the handle of the RPG. With his dying breath, he launched the grenade. The explosive projectile streaked between the two buildings.

Caine had less than a second to duck back behind the wall.

The deafening explosion made his ears ring. The air reverberated around him as the concussion wave hit. A fireball ignited nearby and dust clogged the air.

Opening his eyes, Caine wondered why he wasn't dead. His ears were still ringing. His room seemed mostly intact. The man had missed.

Part of the concrete floor gave way and crumbled, creating a gaping void beneath him. Then another section fell away. His room was disintegrating around him.

The rocket must have hit the floor below, he realized.

Caine sprinted while the ground collapsed under his feet. He leapt for the door, just as the floor disappeared. He threw himself forward, his fingers barely finding purchase on the edge of the concrete slab that seconds ago had held his bed.

He hung there for several seconds, as the dust cleared and the floors gave way below him. Three floors below had crumbled into rubble, no doubt crushing whoever had occupied the lower rooms. His pack still hung off his back, and the AK-47 remained strapped over his shoulder.

The large concrete slab beneath him hung at a steep angle, propped up against the wall. Caine heard the building foundations groan. He knew he had only seconds before the entire building collapsed. He let go, dropped onto the slab, and slid thirty feet down until he hit the rubble below. He stumbled outside, just in time. The remains of the hotel disintegrated behind him. He coughed and lurched away, as a cloud of dust flew up from the rubble.

Ejecting the empty banana shaped magazine from the AK, Caine slapped in another one. He pulled back on the charging handle. As he advanced into the street, he ignored the terrified stares of late night pedestrians. He kept his eyes on the roof of the building across from the destroyed hotel.

Another man with an AK-47 of his own peered over the edge of the roof. Caine put a bullet in his head, killing him instantly. He squeezed the trigger for another rapid fire burst to deter anyone else up there from peering down. Then he darted down the street, and vanished into the crowds. He didn't care that he carried an AK-47 openly. Half the people on the street were as armed as he was.

Caine jogged down a dark alley, while wrapping the scarf around his head like a turban, leaving only his eyes showing. Then he pulled on the thoob, so he looked the part of a Yemeni man. As he marched ahead, he was careful not to trip or cut himself on the debris littering the alley's floor. He stepped through a pack of chittering rats scavenging for food. The scent in the air was a mixture of cordite and raw sewage.

He should have called in, but his instincts said it was better that everyone thought he was dead now. Plus, if Delbridge was correct, and there was a traitor inside the CIA, the Embassy was the last place he should go.

He checked his satellite phone. He knew he should have dumped it, but without it he had no way of knowing where he was in this country. So he compromised. He used Google Maps to work out the best route to Taiz and Ring Road, and from there the best route to Kimberley Hustwait's apartment. Then he removed the battery and SIM card, and kept walking.

The meeting spot was a forty-minute walk. Caine kept in the shadows, wary of another ambush. This was easier than expected because few street lights worked. The dark streets were empty and devoid of crowds... fewer people were out and about in this part of town.

He spotted Delbridge standing on the corner of the road, bathed in one of the few working lights. A line of blood ran across his forehead, and trickled down the side of his face. The CIA man looked concussed. The blow to the head had rattled him. That might have explained why he was standing in such an obvious position.

Caine made a hissing noise, which immediately caught Delbridge's attention.

The two men made eye contact. A second later, two gunshots fired from the shadows.

Two bloody holes opened in Delbridge's chest.

The CIA Station Head staggered for a moment, then fell to his knees.

Caine readied the AK, and scanned the shadows across the street, looking for the shooter. He saw nothing.

A van screeched across the road, stopped in front of Delbridge's corpse. The large vehicle blocked Caine's view.

Caine fired, but his shots ricocheted off the sides... the vehicle was armored.

The van's engine roared, and its tires squealed. It pulled away, and raced off into the darkness.

Delbridge was nowhere to be seen. Whoever was in the armored van, they had taken his body with them.

CHAPTER THIRTEEN

Caine marched at a rapid pace through the war-torn city, taking the route he'd memorized to Kimberley's apartment. His senses were buzzing, and he was hyperaware of his surroundings. Monochromatic sedans and four-wheel drives sped past him on the narrow streets. A group of men wearing thoobs and futa skirts swaggered by. Several women, garbed head to toe in black abaya, shuffled down a decrepit footpath. None paid him any mind.

At one point, a Soviet Union era BTR-60 armored personnel carrier rumbled down the street. A Yemeni soldier manned the roof-mounted machine gun, but even he didn't appear to notice Caine.

Despite his success at blending in with the crowd, the feeling that he was being watched was unrelenting. He performed several surveillance detection routes. He made abrupt stops, pretending to tie the laces on his boots, or pausing to read a poster in Arabic. Each time he waited for someone in the crowd to reveal that they were watching him. But so far, no one aroused his suspicion.

He picked up his pace, and finally arrived at Kimberley's apartment. Her building was a rundown, five story apartment block made of old concrete. Caine picked the front lock in under a minute, then ascended the stairs until he reached the fifth floor. He found Kimber-ley's apartment number, and pounded on the door with his fist. It was after midnight, and he doubted she would be expecting anyone at this hour. He wondered if she would answer.

"Who is it?" she called from behind the locked door.

"Matthew. Matthew Quinn."

"From the Embassy?"

"Yes. Can I come in?"

He heard fumbling with the lock. The door opened a fraction of an inch, held in place by a security chain.

"What are you doing here, and at this hour?" she asked, glaring at him through the tiny space.

"I need to speak to you, it's urgent. But I can't talk out here."

Her eyes widened as she took in the AK-47 strapped across his back, and the turban and thoob he was wearing. "I don't think so."

She tried to slam the door in his face, but his boot was already blocking it. He knew he was scaring her, and he could ill afford to get on her bad side now. It was time to reveal more about who he really was. He had to build some trust between them.

"Kimberley, please, listen. I'm not with Immigration and Customs Enforcement. I'm with the CIA."

"I knew it," she mumbled.

"You've stumbled into a covert operation. I have to get you out of here right now. You're not safe here. People are coming. Dangerous people."

"You look pretty dangerous right now," she said, looking him up and down. "How do I know you're not here to kill me?"

"If I was, I would have shot you already. There's no need to be subtle in this country."

In the distance, another explosion detonated.

It sounded close.

They both stared at each other for a moment, transfixed, as if waiting for a second bomb to fall on them.

"Here," he said, and passed her his pistol, grip first. "Take this.

You can keep it pointed at me while we talk if it makes you feel better. But we do need to talk."

She nodded, took the weapon, and closed the door. He heard her unlatching the chain, then she opened it again and let him in. She held the pistol in her hand, but it hung in a loose grip by her side.

The apartment was dark, lit only by candles. The tiny living quarters smelled of sweat and unwashed clothes. The stifling heat of the day was trapped inside, suggesting the space enjoyed little ventilation. He noticed a woman towards the back of the apartment in an abaya. She quickly covered her face, but not fast enough... Caine recognized her as the woman in the satellite imagery. The Bedouin rider, traveling alone in the heart of the Empty Quarter.

"What's this about, Matthew?" Kimberly demanded.

Caine nodded to the second woman. "Your friend here, she saw an airplane go down in the desert three and a half weeks ago. That plane contained highly classified material. Both the CIA and the Saudi military believe she has it now. Whatever it is, they're willing to kill to stop those secrets from getting out."

The desert woman spoke to Kimberley in rapid Arabic. Kimberley responded just as fluently. Caine tried to follow what they were saying. He could tell they were discussing who he was, a spy that might be dangerous. Kimberley didn't seem to think he was the enemy. The rest was lost on him.

Caine's head jerked to the window, as several vehicles screeched to a sudden stop outside. He pushed past both women and peered through the grilled window at the street below. Men with AK-47s clambered out of three battered utility vehicles. One of them pointed to Kimberly's apartment block, and shouted to his comrades. Caine grabbed Kimberly by the arm, and pulled her to the side of the window. She peered down at the scene in the street.

"Believe me now?" he muttered.

"This could be a set up." Kimberley countered.

Caine grimaced. The Australian woman was suspicious. It would be difficult to convince her he was on her side, and right now he didn't have time to argue. He could force them both to leave with him, but that strategy wouldn't help him in the long run.

"Fine. I'm going downstairs, stealing a car, and getting out of here. You can both come with me, or you can take your chances with those men outside."

He turned and took the stairs, descending only one floor. He waited only a minute before Kimberley and her friend followed. Kimberley carried a small backpack. When the desert woman pointed to Kimberly's exposed face, she covered up with her own veil. Caine nodded when they reached him. He moved forward, his AK-47 out and ready. He heard the two women's quiet footsteps on the stairs behind him.

Once on the ground, Caine and the women hid in the shadows between the buildings. He watched the insurgents as they loitered outside, arguing what to do. They didn't seem in a hurry to raid the apartment building.

"Do you have a car?" he whispered to Kimberley.

"In a garage, just around the corner," she hissed back.

"Good, let's go."

They left the grounds through a back alley, and made their way around the corner to the garage. Soon they were in Kimberley's two door Fiat 126 sedan. The tiny vehicle was cramped, and Caine's head scraped against the roof. He let Kimberley drive, figuring she knew the city better than he did. The Bedouin woman squeezed into the back.

With his field pack wedged at his feet, and his AK-47 resting on his chest, he didn't have much room to move. The engine struggled and wheezed as they drove down the street. Caine considered the benefits of finding a faster, larger vehicle. But they were moving, and no one was following. An alternative car would have to wait.

"My name is Matthew Quinn," he said in faltering Arabic to the woman in the back. "Can I ask what your name is?"

The two women laughed.

"What's so funny?" he asked first in English, then Arabic.

"Your Arabic's not terrible, but it's not great either." Kimberley grinned. "Just stick with English and I'll translate. Oh, and her name is Safiya Naaji by the way. We have an agreement, her and I. We'll help you if you help us."

"Is that right?"

"Damn straight it is."

They turned onto a major road, heavy with trucks and night traffic. Soon they were speeding east, out of the city.

"And how exactly am I supposed to help you?" Caine asked.

"Her husband was killed by mercenaries, the same men who kidnapped her sons. If you return her sons to her safely, she promises to take you to the crashed airplane."

Caine nodded. "Alright. Tell Ms. Naaji we have a deal."

CHAPTER FOURTEEN

Kimberley drove her Fiat out of Sana'a's congested nighttime traffic, and through the Central Highland mountains. In the early hours of the morning, as the sun rose ahead in the east, they hit the Al Qaeda controlled 'checkpoints' in the township of Ma'rib.

Caine spoke to the heavily armed guards, using practiced phrases Safiya had taught him earlier. He explained they were Bedouin, returning from a trip to Sana'a where they had sold rugs. He was the only one talking, since Al Qaeda didn't deem to speak to women. His story was that Safiya was his wife and Kimberley was his daughter. The aid worker's age was close to his own, but that didn't matter. With all but her eyes covered, no one could tell her real age at a glance.

Caine's weapons were never once questioned.

After a few minutes of awkward negotiation, he paid their 'protection' money. The guards let them through.

By early morning they entered the desert. The sun climbed higher in the sky, and soon they were deep within the dunes of the world's largest sand desert. Most of the sand rifts were more than two-hundred feet high. When they stopped for a break, Caine stared north towards the heart of the Empty Quarter. They had parked on a rise, and all he could see were wave after wave of dunes. The towering mounds stretched a hundred miles or more, and vanished beyond the horizon. A thousand aircraft could crash into that desert and none would ever be found again. He felt humbled by the vast expanse before him.

"It's impressive," Kimberley said as she came up behind him.

"It is," he agreed.

"These dunes are tiny, compared to what we'll find deeper in."

"You've been inside the Empty Quarter?"

She shook her head. "I've travelled further north than this, but I've only stood on its edge. Those dunes move by the way, up to thirty meters a year."

"So, you can't even use them as landmarks?"

"That's right. They're like waves in the sea, only in slow motion."

Caine squinted in the harsh, over-head sun. He turned to look back at her. "How do you know so much about the Quarter?"

Kimberley shrugged. "I don't know. I like to immerse myself in the history of the places I visit. The geography, the culture. There is much that is beautiful about this country. The Empty Quarter is beautiful in my eyes, as well."

He looked out again over the endless sea of burning sands. "I agree with you," he said, shading his eyes with his hands. "It is beautiful. Beautiful and dangerous. Like a tiger, or a leopard."

She laughed but said nothing.

"We should get going," he said. "So far no one's followed us, but that doesn't mean we aren't being hunted."

They left quickly. Caine took a turn driving, with Kimberley in the seat next to him providing direction. Safiya, being the smallest of the three, again squeezed into the back.

While they drove, Kimberly translated as Safiya told her story to Caine. Her trek across the Rub' al Khali. How she had found the plane, loaded with American weapons. Her plan to sell the arms to buy food, medicine and protection from Al Qaeda. Safiya burst into tears as she described how her husband had been murdered before her very eyes. Her sobbing grew more intense as she told Caine about her sons... how they were taken as hostages by the mercenaries.

Caine grilled her on the men who had attacked her camp. What did they look like? What weapons did they carry? What languages did they speak? Anything he could think of that might help him find them. She answered as best she could, but he had to rely on Kimberley to translate back and forth.

Finally, Kimberly relayed Safiya's demands to Caine. "She wants you to find her children first, before she takes you to the aircraft wreckage."

"I'm sorry." Caine shook his head. "I would like to, I really would, but we have no leads. The aircraft you described, it must be the DHC-6 Twin Otter I'm looking for. The people who took your children want whatever is hidden on that plane. If we can get to the plane first, we can use what we find there to negotiate Mohammad's and Hussein's release. For all the children's release."

Safiya fired off a rapid string of Arabic words. Caine couldn't grasp any of what she was saying, so he looked to Kimberley for help.

"She doesn't believe you. She says you're an American, and American's only look after themselves."

He gritted his teeth, frustrated that the two women did not yet trust him. "I've promised to find her children. And I will."

Kimberley shook her head. "We want to believe you. But actions speak louder than words."

Caine sighed. He knew if the situation was reversed, he wouldn't believe his offer either. He turned to Kimberley, and said, "Why are you wrapped up in this anyway? I thought UN workers weren't supposed to get involved in individual cases?"

Kimberley waved her hand out the window, letting the passing air cool her arm. "Yes, that's what we were told. But that's not me. I know I can't help everyone, but sometimes you have to help one person. Sometimes improving one person's life can make things better for everyone. Besides, you see what it's like here... how can I just look away?"

Caine nodded. "You're right."

She looked surprised. "You agree with me?"

"I do, actually. I came to Yemen because my friend was killed."

"I'm sorry to hear that, but how does that relate?"

Caine paused, gathered his thoughts. "She knew that sensitive information was on the downed aircraft. And she was killed for what she knew. I might not be able to help her anymore, but I came here to find the men who killed her. That led me to you, and Safiya. So in a way, she's the reason I'm here helping both of you."

"Maybe... "

"We're in this together, Kimberley. Our goals are aligned. You're searching for missing cholera and malaria medicine. Safiya is searching for her sons. I'm searching for a missing plane, and intel that might reveal my friend's killers. What if all our searches lead to the same place, a common enemy? We should help each other. Maybe that's how we make things better for everyone."

"How?"

If we work together, we can find the children, and return the medicines. And when I find the people who killed my friend..." His voice trailed off. He glared at the dusty road and empty dunes ahead.

He turned, and caught Kimberley staring at him. He gripped the wheel tighter.

"Look," he said, turning back to face the road, "if we leave Safiya's children with those mercenaries, they'll either end up dying, or be sold into slavery. Or maybe they're used as child soldiers, and then the next cycle of violence begins. Same with the medicines. They can bring hope to people who have lost everything, including their health. My friend died, but that doesn't mean something good can't come out of all of this."

Safiya sobbed again, and her body shook as her tears intensified.

Caine wanted to comfort her but he didn't know how, so Kimberley and he drove in silence, and let her be. Kimberley was correct. There were no words that could sooth her. Only actions would heal her now.

By midday a small township appeared in the distance. The tiny buildings stood against a rock outcrop skirting the desert sands. The majority of buildings were mud brick. But as they drew closer, a few modern buildings appeared in the center of town, including a gas station.

"You should fill up," Kimberley reminded him. "Not sure there will be another petrol station for a while."

Caine agreed and pulled up to a pump. Stepping out, the hot naked sun beat down on him, causing him to sweat. He dusted off the sand that built up on everything. He could even taste it in the air.

When Kimberley and Safiya stepped out of the car, he said, "Don't wander too far."

He couldn't read Kimberley's expression through her veil, but he sensed she wasn't impressed with his instruction.

"There's a shop over there," she said, pointing to a concrete building that looked more like a bunker than a retail establishment. "Safiya and I are going to purchase some provisions. It's going to be expensive out here, so you're paying."

She put her hands out and he gave her money.

"Don't you wander too far," she said, winking.

Caine laughed. "I'll give you fifteen minutes, then I'll come looking for you."

Kimberley shrugged and the two women walked away from him. From behind, draped in their shapeless abayas, he could only distinguish the two by Kimberley's taller frame.

A man came out to unlock the pump. Caine asked that he fill the tank and provide him with three gas cans. When he was satisfied that the job was done, he paid with cash and returned to the Fiat.

Kimberley and Safiya had not yet returned. It was hot in the car, so he leaned against the vehicle, and watched the buildings of the small town.

His eyes drifted to another concrete building, about two-hundred feet down the road. Thin people lingered outside, many with even thinner, emaciated children hanging off their arms. A slumped, listless woman cradled a crying baby in a loose embrace. The infant's belly was bloated from malnutrition, and he had no meat on his spindly limbs.

Caine couldn't help himself. He stepped towards the makeshift building. As he walked closer, the stench became awful. The air smelled of sweat and human excrement. Men, women and children all looked up at him, their pitiful eyes sunk deep into their sockets. Some put out their hands for money. Many were too tired to do even that.

He walked closer. He looked down and saw another mother cradling the corpse of a child in her stick-thin arms. Caine gritted his teeth. There was no doubt... these people were infected with cholera. There was no medicine here to save them.

He stormed back to the Fiat. Safiya and Kimberley were waiting for him, carrying bags with food.

"What's up?" Kimberley asked.

"My friend," Caine muttered, his voice an angry growl. "I owe her... owe her my life. But she's part of this. Stealing medicine. Letting people suffer." His fists clenched and unclenched. The need to punch something grew overwhelming.

"So, what are you going to do about it?" Kimberley demanded.

Caine paused. He bit down on his anger and let his training kick in. He calmed his breathing, assessed his situation, and formulated a plan. He knew what he had to do.

"I'm going to do what I promised. We need to move out, now!"

CHAPTER FIFTEEN

RIYADH, RIYADH REGION, SAUDI ARABIA

Sulieman Rashid was once proud that he owned a spacious home in Saudi Arabia's capital. His house was one of the few large enough to feature a built in swimming pool. High walls and date palms provided shade, and ensured no one could see inside, so the pool could be used by his whole family. It was Friday today, the weekend. Everyone was home. His two teenage sons played in the pool while he sat on a lounge chair in his swim suit, watching over them.

His daughter wore her black Abaya, but left her face uncovered. She brought him a mint tea, like they made in Morocco. He thanked her and Allah for the refreshment. That seemed to please her. She asked if she could do anything else for him, but he said no, and thanked her again. She bowed and shuffled away, off to help her mother with the chores and housework.

He watched his two sons wrestle in the pool. The older one pushed his younger brother under over and over again, trying to scare him. Pretending to drown him.

Rashid knew he should intervene, but he didn't. He didn't care. He didn't care about anything.

He tried to imagine how he would feel if he had to disappear, if his arrangement with Jarod Forster and the CIA was revealed to the public. Secretly, the Saudi Arabian Government didn't want medicines inside Yemen. They had sanctioned this operation. His superiors had even laid the groundwork, implicating the Iranian-backed Houthis for hijacking UN pharmaceuticals. They hoped to turn the world against their uprisings. The only problem facing Rashid was if the mission became public. If the kickbacks he and his CIA partner received, for the sales of the illicit goods in the United Arab Emirates, were revealed. He had made a significant profit already, enough to buy a villa in faraway Marrakesh. If his corruption ever came to light, he could run and disappear there. His only question was, should he bring his family with him?

If he ran and left his family in Riyadh, they would suffer. His wife and children would be treated as traitors, forced to live on the streets as beggars. His wife and daughter would no doubt be raped. His sons might even be executed. How could they not? It would be assumed that they were complicit in his deception, even though they knew nothing of what he did. Could he let that happen to them? Would Allah forgive him for such a course of action?

He just didn't care.

Four years ago, before the Mossad agent had impaled his brain with a knife, he would have done anything to protect his family. Anything to remain pious in the eyes of Almighty God. Now, he just didn't care. He knew he should, but he didn't. If others suffered because he abandoned them, well that wasn't his concern. He couldn't feel hurt, or sadness, or... anything.

Yes, if he needed to run, he could. No emotional ties would hold him back.

His phone rang.

The call was unlisted but he answered anyway.

"It's me," said the electronically distorted voice.

"Yes?" Rashid had decided earlier that he would keep his responses short. Let the American do all the talking.

"Just wanted to let you know, our Station Head was murdered last night," he said, referring to Martin Delbridge without actually using his name. "The one man who could have connected you and I is no longer in the equation."

"Yes?" Rashid replied in a monotone voice.

"Yes? What the fuck does 'yes' mean? I thought you'd be over the fucking moon about that?"

Rashid said nothing.

"What is it? You can't talk? Why did you fucking answer then?"

"I can talk." Rashid stepped away from the pool as he wrapped a towel around his waist. He walked into the men's bathroom. He needed privacy if he were to answer in more than just single words.

If he had emotions, Rashid knew he would be feeling frustration right now. His hacker, Mansoor Alharbi, had been unable to locate where Jarod Forster was hiding out. The CIA man had conveniently faked his own death. No one in his own organization was looking for him. There were no leads from other spy agencies he could hack into.

Forster's faked death had complicated matters, but it would only be a matter of time before Alharbi found him. Then Rashid would send a kill team to watch over Forster. They would stand ready to assassinate his partner when he gave the command. There were enough loyal men under him who would do the job willingly and without question.

The American continued speaking. "Well my friend, before you go and get all excited, brace yourself for even better news?"

Again, Rashid said nothing.

"For fuck sake, I'm out on a limb here!" the American exclaimed.

"Just tell me what you have done."

The American laughed, an odd crackle through the voice distorting software. "Our man on the ground is isolated. He doesn't trust his own people. He's teamed up with a local woman who might know where the missing plane went down. We're following him.

When he finds the plane, that's when either you or I, or both of us, tie up the last of the loose ends. We'll make it a nice, neat little bow."

Rashid thought about what he was being told. The key here was the data stick on the downed aircraft. What he and the American were doing was authorized by his government, but it had to remain a secret. If the files got out, it could spark a war between their two governments. If that happened, Rashid knew he would be the first casualty, punished with a bullet in the back of his head.

Neither side wanted a war. The data stick had to be destroyed at all costs. If what Forster had just told him was true, then maybe life could continue as it was. Pleasant. Comfortable. Numb.

"Very well," Rashid replied. "Let me know when this man is close to the crash site. I'll send in a team to clean up."

"Good. I'll have drones in the air to support you. I'm glad we're still on the same page on this one."

"Oh, we are."

"I'll call when I have more news."

The line went dead.

Rashid stood motionless for a minute, knowing that another call was not far away. When his phone rang, it was also unlisted. He answered simply with a "Yes?"

"It's me," said Alharbi. The hacker's voice was a nervous stutter. It had been explained very clearly to him what would happen if he didn't provide the information Rashid needed. One of his sons would have an unfortunate accident, in the very near future.

"Did you find what I need?" Rashid asked.

Alharbi swallowed. "I did," he said. "Forster is in Sana'a."

"Where in Sana'a exactly?"

"You won't believe me when I tell you. Forster's inside the U.S. Embassy."

Rashid found himself contemplating this news. If he had emotions, what would they be right now?

He had nothing.

So he simply said, "That's very interesting, indeed."

CHAPTER SIXTEEN

THE EMPTY QUARTER, AL JAWF GOVERNORATE, YEMEN

Sand.

Everything was sand.

The tiny grains blew around their feet when standing. Luckily, the swirling sand didn't reach them when they were perched up high, riding on camels. Even when the howling winds picked up, few grains rose higher than a few feet above the dunes.

But the sand bothered Caine less than the heat. For three days Safiya had led them deep into the driest, hottest, most inhospitable sand desert on the planet. During the day the temperature never dropped below a hundred. There was no shade, nowhere to go to get away from the burning sun. They were always thirsty, but they had to conserve their water rations, to ensure they made it to the next oasis.

They travelled by night, when it was cooler. Safiya explained how she used the Great Bear constellation to guide them towards Polaris, the northern star. The facing of the dunes was another guide she used to keep them headed in the right direction... The towering mounds of sand formed perpendicular to the eastern blowing winds. Caine had his satellite phone, and could have guided them by GPS. But he decided it was safer to trust Safiya's traditional Bedouin ways. A satellite phone could be tracked, giving away their position. He kept it switched off, with the battery disconnected.

Night time in the desert was strangely peaceful. Caine was struck by how silent and still everything was. This deep into the Empty Quarter, the dunes were five-hundred feet or higher. In the silver moonlight, they looked like ocean waves frozen in time.

When their camels carried them over the crests, Caine could see for what seemed to be hundreds of miles in any direction. The Milky Way above was brilliant in the cloudless sky. He had never seen so many stars. He could even make out the gas clouds that formed the spiral arms of the galaxy. Meteors were plentiful... brief streaks of light on the dark, distant horizon.

The only living creatures they had seen in their travels was a distant herd of Arabian Oryx, two days ago. Safiya told Caine that the desert antelopes took water from the scant vegetation in the area. They would walk hundreds of miles to find the tiniest patch of green. Life in the dunes was harsh, but other than humans, the Oryx had no predators.

From dusk until dawn, their camels grumbled but kept a steady pace. They were covering around twenty-five miles a day. Kimberley had traded her Fiat for the four camels... three to ride and one to carry provisions. The heaviest load they carried were the containers of water. They brought enough to last three humans two weeks. The camels could go without for up to five days between oases. When the animals drank, they would consume up to twenty gallons in one go.

Since their escape from Sana'a there had been no signs anyone was following them. But Caine knew spy satellites and drones could be watching them at any time without them noticing. In an effort to throw pursuers off their track, they all wore the long white tunics, sleeveless cloaks and head cloths of Bedouin men. It had been Safiya's idea. It would be risky if they encountered another Bedouin caravan this deep in the Empty Quarter. But he hoped it would confuse aerial surveillance, should they be spotted.

Riding a camel had taken some getting used to, and it was a challenge just to control them. Caine was a fit man. He could run thirty miles through mountainous terrain without stopping once for a rest. But the unrelenting rolling motion of the camel, and the uncomfortable saddle, left him stiff and sore after hours of riding.

Safiya stopped them in a narrow valley between two high dunes. They would camp here, to minimize the time the sun would be upon them. After quenching their thirst, they erected their tents. The shelters were made of woven goat hair, and supported by poles and guy ropes. This had been Caine's third attempt at erecting a Bedouin tent. He was getting used to the intricacies of its design.

Safiya watched him work. "Did you know that in my culture, it is deemed woman's work to prepare the tent?"

Caine grinned. "Well, where I come from I believe in sharing—" He stopped and looked up at her. "Wait a minute. You speak English?"

With only the three of them, hundreds of miles from anywhere, Safiya no longer hid her face. She stared back at him, but said nothing. Kimberley rested her hands on her hips, and gave him a smug grin.

"So you both lied to me?" Caine asked, as he finished setting up the tent.

"Oh, don't be a sook," Kimberley baited in her Aussie accent. "Tough love 'em and leave 'em bloke like you must be used to lying to women. Now you're surprised when they lie back?"

Caine wiped the sand off his arms and hands, and laughed. "Still don't trust me?"

"We needed to know what kind of man you were," Safiya answered. Whoever had taught her English was from Britain, Caine noted. The woman spoke with an English accent.

"If you didn't think you needed me to translate," Kimberley added, "you might have abandoned me back in Al Abr. There was no way I was letting Safiya travel alone with a strange man deep into the desert—"

"—So we tested you," Safiya added. She was conversing fluidly, as if the two women were starting and ending each other's sentences. "We wanted to see how you reacted at the clinic, with the cholera patients—"

"—And I wanted to see what your reaction was. To see if you actually cared about the plight of women and children in this country."

Caine opened his mouth to speak, but he was lost for words. The two women were a united front, and he knew a losing battle when he saw one. He had to admire their fortitude and principals.

"I gave you my word," he finally said. "I have no intention of breaking it. But if you don't trust me, why are we here?"

"I said we didn't trust you," Kimberley answered. "Past tense. My Aussie bullshit detector is still on, but you've stuck it out this long. Maybe you've got what it takes."

Without warning Safiya began shaking. She started sobbing again. Kimberley held her, gave her comfort. Neither she nor Caine said another word for several minutes.

Safiya's sobbing finally subsided. Caine put an arm on her shoulder. "I promise you again," he said. "I'll do whatever I can to find your children. Whatever it takes."

"Me too," Kimberley said, also placing her hand on her heart. "I promise that too."

Safiya wiped the stray tears from her eyes. Soon the sun would be rising, so she excused herself to climb a dune and face north, ready for her morning prayers.

When Safiya was out of earshot, Kimberley said casually, "Your name isn't really Matthew Quinn, is it?"

"No," he said, just as casually.

"Thought so," she said with a shrug. "You going to tell me?"

"It's Thomas. Thomas Caine."

"Thomas," she said, smiling. "Suits you better than Matthew."

She rummaged through their bags until she found dates, flat bread and coffee. "Hungry? Thirsty?"

"Yes, and yes. I'll get a fire going." They had brought kindling and paraffin oil, enough to brew coffee twice a day. He was surprised she didn't ask him more about who he was, but perhaps that was all she needed... a name. Someone she could trust.

He hoped he wouldn't be forced to let her down.

Kimberley looked up at the dune, where Safiya was bowing down in prayer. "How much danger are we in, Thomas?"

Now that the sun was rising, Caine placed his sunglasses over his eyes. "I really don't know. I was attacked in Sana'a, but since then, nothing. I have to assume someone doesn't want the downed aircraft found. But if we were being followed, I think I would have spotted them by now."

"Is that why you keep looking over your shoulder all the time?"

He nodded. "Occupational hazard."

She glanced back at Safiya. "She's scared, but she hides it well. She believes she'll never see her children ever again. She's afraid you will betray us."

"I know," Caine said thoughtfully. "What do you think?"

"You're an enigma, Thomas Caine. But until you prove other-wise, I trust you'll do what's right. And I'll fight the good fight beside you."

Caine did not reply. He watched Safiya finish her prayers in silence.

CHAPTER SEVENTEEN

THE EMTPY QUARTER, NAJRAN REGION, SAUDI ARABIA

Early into the night they stumbled across a bitumen road stretching into the west. A battered sedan sped past, and disappeared into the distance. Kimberley shuddered. She hadn't expected signs of modern civilization to pop up out of nowhere.

"This is the Khbash to Sharorah Road," Safiya explained. "We are well inside Saudi Arabia now."

"Wow! Really?" Kimberly asked, her voice tinged with anxiety.

She shivered for a second, despite the intense heat. This was her first illegal border crossing. She was now inside one of the least friendly nations on earth for women. She took a deep breath and reminded herself why she was here. She urged her camel on.

Safiya crossed the road first with the cargo camel trailing behind her. Kimberley was next, and Caine took up the rear. Kimberly was still getting used to his real name. When she told Safiya, the Bedouin woman had given her a pensive look, but did not comment. She hadn't seemed at all surprised he'd been using an alias.

In under a minute they were over the road and traversing the next sand dune. Modern infrastructure vanished as quickly as it had appeared.

The quarter moon was luminous in the horizon, bathing the Empty Quarter in dark blues. Despite the constant sense of fore-boding that gripped her, she thought the desert was beautiful. It held mystic, almost supernatural qualities. It's silence and stillness created a sense of peace. That, combined with hours of rocking to the rhythmic pace of her marching camel, led to drifting thoughts. Like waking dreams, they ran through her head. A subconscious analysis of what the hell she was doing, and why she was here.

Life in Sydney had been fun, safe and secure. A good job, great friends, and family who loved her. So why had she uprooted her pros-perous life? Why had she come to work in one of the most dangerous and desperate regions on the planet?

Her answer always sounded corny when she explained it to others. She wanted to make a difference in the lives of those less fortunate than her. It made her feel that her life finally held purpose. She had never felt so satisfied, so complete. Sure, there was the bureaucracy of the UN to deal with. Plus the sexism, the backward practices of Middle Eastern government, made her want to scream at the top of her lungs. But she could also see the results of her labor. Women, children and men lived better lives because of the aid she provided. How many people back home could say the same?

At first she thought that aid work would be something she would do for a few years at the most. Now she wasn't certain she would ever stop.

Caine rode by her and smiled. He was a handsome man. Fit, muscular, and all alpha male. More importantly, he was considerate and respectful. There was a depth to him, something more behind those emerald eyes than selfish needs and desires. The last character-istic was his most attractive trait, but also his most mysterious.

Kimberley felt certain he was a former U.S. Navy SEAL, Delta Force operator, or something similar. A special forces hero who spent most of his life operating behind enemy lines. She'd met a few of their kind over the years in Iraq and Yemen.

Like Caine, they were all quietly confident and rarely bragged. But they never seemed to give much thought to what they were doing. Point and shoot. Fire and forget. Kill a few terrorists in the night, then go and have some beers with some mates and watch the Gridiron. But with Caine, she sensed something more behind his piercing green eyes.

She had seen the way he reacted to the infected masses, in the town on the outskirts of the desert. The look in his eyes when he talked about the death of his friend. The tenderness in his voice, when he promised Safiya that he would find her sons.

She realized that despite his hard exterior, Caine was not indifferent to the suffering of others.

Later in the night when the moon had set, he rode alongside her. "How are you holding up?" he asked.

"Okay, I guess. Scared out of my mind, but okay."

"Well, look on the bright side," he said with a grin. "We've made it this far."

"We made a promise. I never go back on my promises."

"I can see that."

"When I think about what Safiya has gone through—is still going through—I know I have nothing to complain about," she said.

Safiya was ahead by about thirty meters, leading the way. She mostly kept to herself. Kimberley suspected it was because she didn't want them to see how much she was hurting.

Kimberly sighed. "To have a child die is bad enough. But at least then, you know their suffering is at an end. To have them go missing, not knowing what's happening to them, if you'll ever see them again... it would destroy you."

Caine nodded, but said nothing.

She glanced over at him. "Why are you here, Thomas?"

"To find the intel on the missing aircra—"

"No," she said, cutting him off. "I mean... I know your mission, but why do you work for the CIA? You're putting your life on the line too. I'm guessing you do it all the time. There must be some kind of greater purpose, right?"

The man called Caine looked towards the horizon. "I've done a lot of bad things, Kimberley, but I've always thought that what I did served a greater good. I know how that sounds... but it's true. Most of the world is run by bad people. The CIA, our allies... I know they aren't perfect. But things would be worse if they weren't out there in the field, fighting back."

She nodded, not certain that he had answered her question. Like all soldiers she had encountered, he was guarded. She knew with men like him, there would always be aspects of his personality and his past that would remain closed to the rest of the world.

"How does Safiya speak English so well?" he asked, changing the subject.

Kimberley shrugged. "That's quite a story. Safiya told me that as a child, she and her sister discovered an Englishman dying in a jeep. He had crashed, traveling off road in the desert. They rescued the man, and together with her father and mother, they nursed him back to life. But he had broken his back, leaving him a paraplegic. His name was Justin Melville. He was some kind of banker, advising the Saudi Royal Family. Melville had swindled them out of a vast fortune. Before that, he had embezzled money from several of the largest banks in England, so he had nowhere to go. He made a deal with Safiya's father. He taught Safiya and her siblings English and mathematics, in return for food and lodging, and to keep his location secret. I guess life as a cripple in a Bedouin camp was better than a Saudi jail."

Caine grunted. "That's some story. Do you believe it?"

She raised an eyebrow at Caine's suspicious remark. "What has Safiya got to gain from lying?"

"Nothing, I guess. What happened to Melville? Is he still alive?"

"No, she said he died like ten years ago or something. Some kind of fever he never recovered from."

Caine nodded. "One more secret, buried in the sands."

"Thomas, what's going to happen to Safiya, when this is all over? Widows don't fare well in her culture."

"Let's focus on getting her children back first. Then we can focus on her long-term future."

Ahead, Safiya had made a sharp turn, and galloped her camel back to Caine and Kimberley.

"What's up?" Kimberley asked. She could tell by Safiya's frantic expression that whatever she was about to tell them, it was not good news

"A sandstorm is coming! We must prepare. It will be upon us in minutes!"

CHAPTER EIGHTEEN

A wall of sand, like an ominous cliff face a mile high, stretched from one horizon to the other. The frantic, rolling cloud of darkness was lit by occasional flashes of lightning. It churned across the sand, heading straight towards them.

There was nowhere to run.

Caine leapt off his camel and approached Safiya, yelling already because of the noise. "Do we erect the tent?" he asked, ready to do something. He knew they didn't have long. They had to act quickly.

She shook her head. "Too late! I apologize most profoundly. God forgive me, I did not see the warning signs."

"No need to apologize," Kimberley shouted. "Just tell us what to do!"

Safiya nodded. "The biggest danger is sand getting in our throats. Too much and you will drown."

"Charming," Kimberley replied with a shudder.

"First, we must secure the camels. We must hammer a stake into the sand, deep, and tether them too it. Thomas, can you do that?"

Caine nodded. "Sure. I assume they can endure sandstorms?"

"Yes. Camels have a third eyelid. It protects their eyes when the sand is blowing. They can close their nostrils, and they have bushy eyebrows and eyelashes. They will be fine, so long as we are not separated from them."

"And what do we do?" Kimberly asked.

Caine had been trained in desert survival. He was already dousing some clothes with water from the canteen. He wrapped a wet rag around his mouth and nose, then handed one to Kimberly and Safiya. Safiya nodded when she saw what he was doing. "Kimberley, do as Thomas does. Just breathe normally through the cloth."

"You finish with Kimberley," Caine said. "I'll deal with the camels."

He found the equipment he needed, a hammer and stakes, then bashed two stakes deep into the sand. He took the harnesses of each grunting beast, and secured them to the stakes. Then he returned to Safiya and an increasingly anxious Kimberley.

Safiya smiled, and said to Kimberley in comforting tones, "We will be fine. Just do as I say, and we will get through this safely."

Kimberley nodded, even though she looked no less scared than she had a second before. She looked up suddenly. Caine turned too. The sandstorm was almost upon them, a wall of churning sand that seemed to rise all the way up to the stars.

"Quick, now! We must not be separated!" Safiya shouted.

Safiya proceeded to tie a rope around Kimberley's waist and then her own, securing them together. She moved towards Caine with the rope, when a loud, terrified braying rose over the wind. Caine turned and saw that one of the camels had come loose from its mooring.

"Wait here," he shouted. "I'll be right back!" He ran towards the loose camel, grabbing for the rope that dangled from its harness.

The wind grew even more wild and forceful.

Absolute darkness fell over them.

The noise of the storm was terrifying. The whirling sand stung as it bit against exposed skin. The sky lit up for a brief second, as a bolt of lightning crackled above. Then just as quickly it plunged them back into darkness.

Caine pulled his head scarf around his face, protecting his eyes as best he could. He looked for Kimberley and Safiya, but he could not see them in the storm. The two women were tethered together, but they weren't attached to the camels or Caine. The sandstorm was chaotic and disorientating. If either group moved, they might wander apart and become separated.

"Safiya!" Caine cried out, risking an intake of sand. He should have covered his eyes to protect them, but he had to find the two women before he could protect himself. Grains of sand worked their way under his eyelids, causing his eyes to tear and blink. "Kimberley!"

Another flash of lightning. For a second, he saw the two women. They were huddled together struggling to remain upright in the howling winds. Then everything was plunged into darkness yet again.

Sand was building up around his feet. The wind threatened to blow him over. "Safiya!" he called out again.

Using only touch, he reached into the saddlebags and felt for the guy ropes. When he had one, he tied one end to the camel stake, then the other around his hand. Then he stood, waited for the next flash of lightning. His eyes burned so he kept them squeezed almost closed, but not quite.

When the next bolt came, he saw Kimberley and Safiya standing where he expected them, desperately trying to hold onto each other. He advanced quickly with his eyes closed, pushing against the wind until he smacked into them. He reached out and grabbed one of the women's wrists, then pulled her close. He took the rest of the rope and wrapped it tight around her waist.

"We're all tethered now, including to the camels," he yelled through the stinging sand. "We're safe."

"We need to sit with our backs to the sand," Safiya cried. "Wait out the storm. Also, we are at the bottom of a dune. Sand will build up on us during the night, so we need to keep digging ourselves out. We cannot let it bury us."

Kimberley sobbed. Caine grabbed her and felt her tremble in his arms. He had never seen her this scared, not even during the violence in Sana'a.

The three of them huddled together. Caine kept his arms around both of them. Their head scarfs were wrapped tightly around their faces, protecting their eyes and ears. The only sound they could hear was the howling wind, surging around them. The only sensation they could feel was sand grinding against their skin, penetrating even the tiniest opening in their clothing.

The sandstorm lasted hours. No one spoke. Safiya and Kimberley sobbed from loss and fear respectively. There was nothing Caine could do to comfort either of them, except to hold them tight through the long night of terror.

CHAPTER NINETEEN

Kimberley woke up gasping

Nightmares of suffocating and smothering quickly faded. In their place, rays of early morning sunlight beamed down through the cinnamon hazed skies.

She was half buried in the sand. To her surprise, Caine's taut, muscular arm was wrapped around her.

She lay still for a moment, enjoying his touch. She remembered now, the sandstorm had terrified her like nothing before ever had. She didn't know why. She was a surfer and had once come face to face with a bull shark in the Pacific Ocean. She'd been caught in rips, pounded by crashing waves. Neither had scared her as much as the sandstorm had.

Caine had come to her rescue, held her secure through the worst of the storm. He had stayed with her for hours, taking the brunt of the wind against his back.

She thought about reaching out and kissing him, to say thanks, and to show him how she felt. Caine wasn't like other men she'd encountered. She desired to explore him, discover exactly how deep he went.

Rolling on her back, she turned and looked at his strong, handsome face, now sporting a thick beard.

He opened his eyes, waking. Those beautiful emerald irises of his seemed to peer deep into her very soul. When he saw her staring back, he smiled. "It's over now. Are you okay?"

She didn't think. She just leaned forward and kissed him, hard.

She kept her mouth planted on his, exploring the saltiness of his lips.

Then she realized that he wasn't kissing back.

"I'm so sorry!" Consumed with shame, she pulled away and sat up and turned her back on him.

"Don't be," he said kindly.

"I thought... I thought you felt the same?"

"I do," he said, placing a hand on her back. "It's just... "

She turned to face him, not ready to believe what should have been obvious from the onset. "You have a girlfriend?"

Caine shrugged. "It's complicated."

Kimberley stood, arms folded, and walked from him. She was crying and hadn't realized it. Before anyone noticed, she wiped her tears.

"Can we..." She choked on her words, feeling like she was fifteen again kissing her first boy. Every person she had dated or kissed since university had pursued her. There had never been doubt about whether a guy was interested in her or not. But with Caine, he wasn't like other men. She was chasing him. "Can we pretend this never happened?"

He walked over to her. "I'm in a complicated relationship. It would be unfair to lead you on, and pretend that I am not."

She nodded and looked away before she was teary again. "I'm sorry."

"Don't be."

Desperate to change the subject, Kimberley looked around. Safiya was checking on the camels. Kimberley counted four, all of them grunting and complaining, but otherwise unharmed. She cringed, wondering if Safiya had witnessed her embarrassing rejection.

"I've made coffee," Safiya explained as she approached, acting as if nothing had happened. "And there are dates and bread for breakfast. I'm going to pray, then we should be on our way."

Caine nodded. "Thanks Safiya. I don't know what we would do without you."

She smiled, took her rug and climbed the nearest dune.

Kimberley couldn't shake her embarrassment. Now Thomas Caine knew how she felt about him, and how weak she was. She wanted to run and never talk to him again, until she realized that was the reaction of a fifteen-year-old girl. She wasn't a child anymore. She had to deal with this like an adult.

She noticed what might be uncertainty edging into Caine's expression. He touched the back of his neck. He gazed at the tops of the dunes encircling them.

"What's up?" she asked, glad that they had something else to talk about.

"I don't know," he said. He rubbed the back of his neck. "Just a feeling. Something's not right."

"You get these feelings a lot?"

He nodded.

"What happened the last time you got one?"

"My friend and I were ambushed. She was killed."

Kimberley nodded. She found her binoculars in her pack and looked to Caine. "We should take a look then."

"Agreed."

Caine unwrapped his assault rifle from its protective goat-hair cloth, then checked it to ensure it still worked. The mechanism was clean and sand free.

He hefted the weapon over his shoulder. "Let's go."

They climbed the same dune Safiya was praying on, but kept their distance so as not to disturb her. The dune was about two-hundred meters high. The climb was hard work. The sand kept collapsing around their feet, making their progress feel like two steps forward and one back. When they reached the top, they felt the beginnings of another hot and debilitating day in a roasting desert.

Thousands upon thousands of sand dunes stretched before them, rippling towards the horizon in every direction. The contrast this early in the day between the shadows and the light was stark. She knew the haze in the distance was caused by suspended sand particles left over from the storm. Ripples of wispy clouds decorated the skies, and slivers of bright blue were starting to pierce the fading orange tint. In all her travels, she had never seen anything as beautiful or as scary as the Rub' al Khali.

His binoculars raised, Caine scanned the horizon while she looked north. She saw a tiny sliver of light, as bright as a fallen star. She blinked. Something was reflecting back the sunlight.

"Look over there," she said, pointing.

Caine followed her direction, and looked through the binoculars. He lowered them and grinned. "Take a look yourself."

Kimberley raised her own binoculars. Within a few seconds, she found the anomaly. The tail of an aircraft, perhaps five or six kilometers distant, jutted from the crest of a dune. "It's the plane! The sandstorm must have exposed it during the night."

"My thoughts exactly. Good eye, Kimberley."

When Safiya had completed her prayers, they regrouped. Normally they would set up camp and sleep during the day, but Caine and Safiya both wanted to push on. The plane could disappear again. Better to reach it now than wait until night and lose it forever.

They set off on their camels. The heat became stifling and draining. Kimberley drank her water faster than she should. Caine kept looking behind him, like he was worried they were being followed. If he saw anyone, he didn't mention it to her. Kimberley didn't notice anyone following them either.

After half an hour, they reached the dune crest before the one ahead with the half-buried wreckage. Caine looked down though his binoculars again.

"That's it. The tail number matches the plane I'm looking for. Well done, both of you."

"Let's check the wreckage," Safiya said quickly, "then we can set up camp while we search it."

"Sounds like a plan," Kimberley added, feeling confident again. The lingering memory of her early morning embarrassment was beginning to fade.

They started down the sand dune.

From nowhere, a bright arc of yellow light streaked across the sky.

A split second later, the aircraft exploded.

Kimberly felt a tremor rumble through the sand. A fireball of searing red and orange erupted from the wreckage, disintegrating it utterly. Nothing was left except a burning, blackened hull and a trail of dark smoke spewing up into the sky.

Caine leapt off his camel, and peered up at the skies.

"What happened?" Kimberley asked as she took a deep breath. Her newfound confidence evaporated in an instant.

"Drone!" Caine exclaimed. "It fired a missile at the plane. Split up, because we could be next."

CHAPTER TWENTY

Caine sprinted, AK ready as he scrambled over the dune. The mound of sand didn't provide much protection, but it was the only cover he had against another drone strike. He watched as Safiya and Kimberley did the same, spreading out so the drone would have to pick them off one at a time. Caine knew it probably had sufficient missiles to complete the job. And if the pilot was patient, he could wait until they regrouped, and take them out with a single shot. Against such a foe, there was nowhere they could run.

As the seconds and minutes passed, Caine realized fire from above wasn't coming for them.

Then he noticed the camels. They seemed more agitated than usual. They huddled as a group, grunting in fear and confusion.

Another flash of yellow light ripped through the skies.

The camels didn't know what hit them. In an instant they were burned to a crisp, and blown into a thousand meaty pieces.

The drone didn't need to kill us, Caine thought. The pilot had now effectively stranded them in the desert. Without camels they would die of thirst before they could walk out of there.

Caine scanned the skies, looking for sunlight reflecting off the aircraft's metal skin. He considered who might have sent the unmanned drone. With a sinking feeling in his gut, he realized the Saudis and the Yemeni didn't own aircraft this sophisticated. It had to be one of his own people. Someone inside the CIA wanted the secrets of the downed DHC-6 Twin Otter to remain hidden forever.

No wonder they hadn't encountered resistance during their journey here. Caine had inadvertently led the enemy to the Otter. Now they could finish him off, and destroy the plane once and for all.

There was no other option. He had to call for help.

Caine reached for his satellite phone... only to find his pocket was empty. He realized, with horror, he had either dropped the phone, or it had been lost in the sandstorm. All he had now was a spare battery in his cargo pants.

He muttered a curse. Now they really were in a hopeless situation. They wouldn't see the missile coming. He felt the blood thunder in his temples, and he knew that death was not far away. Not just his own, but Safiya and Kimberley's death as well.

He counted down the minutes. When half an hour passed, he began to think that the drone wouldn't bother with them. Heat and dehydration would be their final executioners.

"What the bloody hell happened?" Kimberley called across the sands, her voice still quavering in fear. "Where is it?"

"Where is what?" Safiya called out

"A drone," Caine shouted. "It took out the plane, then the camels."

"American?" Safiya asked.

Caine nodded. He couldn't think of a plausible alternative.

"Look!" Kimberley pointed across the dunes. Three Humvee military trucks traversed the sand on a beeline towards their location. Two of the Humvees were armed with machine guns and one with a belt feed grenade launcher. That meant four men per vehicle; a driver, gunner, a radio operator and a commander. All would be heavily armed professional soldiers.

Seen through the binoculars, Caine immediately recognized the insignia as Saudi Arabia.

That must be it, he thought. A conspiracy. The Saudis and the Americans working together, to bury a secret neither side wants exposed.

"What do we do?" Safiya asked.

Caine looked at the two women. He saw the fear consuming each of their faces. There seemed to be only one option. "Do you have your abayas?" he asked.

Both women nodded.

"Change into them. If they wanted to blow us up, the drone would have finished us off by now. We're about to be taken into Saudi custody. This will be uncomfortable for all of us, to say the least. But remember, I'll do everything I can to ensure we're released."

While the women changed, Caine gathered his weapons. He could fight, but that option seemed suicidal. There was no cover in the dunes, and the Saudi weapons were far superior to anything he had. Better to surrender to live to fight another day. Then, on a last-minute whim, he ducked behind the dune out of sight from the Humvees. He buried his pack, which held his SIG P226, along with his knife and some other supplies. The Saudis would have already seen him with the Russian assault rifle so there was no point hiding that.

The Humvees came to a halt on the side of the dune. All three turret mounted weapons spun around, and lined them up in their sights. Five soldiers leapt from the Humvees. The men spread out and raised their Steyr AUG assault rifles, ready to shoot if ordered too.

Caine, Kimberley and Safiya marched down the dune, their hands raised in surrender. When they reached the soldiers, they were forced onto their knees. Head scarfs and niqab face veils were torn away from them. Under the heat of the midday sun, they were patted down and searched one by one. All their possessions were removed, including Caine's AK-47 and spare magazines.

The only item they ignored was the useless battery for Caine's missing satellite phone. He looked up at one of the men searching him, a sergeant with big bushy eyebrows as thick as his moustache. Caine was shocked to recognize him as the man who had stared at him in the Indian restaurant, back in Sana'a.

Satisfied, the sergeant turned and gestured to the middle Humvee.

An officer stepped out. He was tall and muscular, with a shaved head and a neatly trimmed beard that was starting to grey. His thick hands looked powerful enough to crack walnuts. His biceps were wider than Caine's calves. A scar ran across the side of his smooth skull, and disappeared around the back of his head. Caine had seen enough such wounds to know it's cause... a deep, near-fatal cut from a combat knife.

Caine recognized the man immediately from the intel files he had studied back at Langley. Colonel Sulieman Rashid, a senior military intelligence officer of the Royal Saudi Land Forces. The reports said that Rashid was based in one of Saudi's missile compounds. He was charged with investigating, interrogating and torturing any employees who might be leaking secrets of the Saudi's missile program.

It was also rumored that Rashid had led numerous covert operations across the Middle East. He had shut down several HUMINT gathering operations in the area, assassinating more than two-dozen CIA and Mossad agents in the process.

"Thomas Caine," he said. He spoke practiced English, in an emotionless monotone. "I suppose I should thank you for leading me to the plane."

Caine focused his stare on Rashid. "You didn't take out the plane yourself. The Americans did, with one of their drones. You're working with my people, aren't you."

Rashid forced his lips into a thin smile. "You are trying to turn my own soldiers against me, Caine. Make them think I have been reduced to an American puppet." He paced around Caine in a tight circle. "It won't work. You fail to understand this is a sanctioned operation, approved by both our governments. My men already know this. We don't want the world to know about it, of course, hence the need to maintain secrecy."

"So you used the Houthi rebels as scapegoats, right? Framed them for stealing medicines from the Yemeni people?"

He grinned again. His smile appeared strained, and Caine sensed it was difficult for the man to express any emotion, even smug victory. It was like he was forcing himself to gloat.

Caine had read that several years back, Rashid had been stabbed in the base of his skull, hence the scar. Rashid should have died. Yet here he was. Caine didn't know how he had managed to survive. But the lasting mental and physical trauma from a wound like that could change a man in many ways... none of them good.

"Yes, Mister Caine, you are correct. They said you were a good agent. I can see why. It is a pity your own CIA betrayed you. Led you into the Empty Quarter as a sacrificial lamb. Well, you've served your purpose now."

"Who are 'they'?"

Rashid paused, then said, "I suppose there's no harm in telling you. After all, you won't live out the day. My contact is Jarod Foster. He tricked you, didn't he? Led you to believe he died when the plane was shot down. He's fooled all of us, but don't worry... I'll find him."

Caine paused. He hadn't considered this possibility. He'd made assumptions based on what he learned from Emily Argyle. But Forster had duped her from the start. Suddenly, a large dimension of this mystery made sense. "So it was Forster who took out Delbridge?"

"Yes, of course."

"You said you had to find him? Why is Forster hiding from you, if you two are partners?"

"If this goes wrong, if we are exposed, Forster needs to understand that I can expose him too."

Rashid nodded to two of his soldiers, one of them being the sergeant with the thick facial hair. He rattled off some instructions in Arabic. Caine couldn't understand his orders, but he watched the men salute and split up. They trudged off through the sand, heading towards the smoldering wreckage and the dead camels.

Then Rashid turned back to Caine. "If Iran thinks they can claim new Persian territory in the Arabian Peninsula, using subversive groups like the Houthis, they are very much mistaken. By framing them for the stolen medicine, we prevent their cause from gaining sympathy. You came all this way to die, just so both our governments could plug a minor leak in a sanctioned operation."

"So what happens to us now?" Caine asked.

Rashid took a moment to consider his response. He watched the soldiers in the distance, combing through the sand.

"I could just shoot the three of you in the back of the head," he finally said, again with no emotion whatsoever. "That is the simplest solution. But my men are tired from driving around the desert searching for this plane. I have promised them that you will suffer for their inconvenience. Leaving you here to die of thirst seems like fitting punishment."

Caine said nothing. It wasn't a great alternative to a fast execution, but far better than being dead. His hand brushed against the satellite phone battery in his pocket. He wondered how he could use that to his advantage. The soldiers had missed it and he wasn't about to remind them of the fact.

The two soldiers returned. The sergeant was carrying Caine's field pack, a large grin etched across his face. Caine's heart sank.

"You were correct sir," he said to Colonel Rashid. "Caine did indeed bury equipment."

"Very good Sergeant Aziz." Rashid looked to Caine again, his expression blank and empty, devoid of any emotion. "I suppose we should be leaving you now."

"Just one more question?"

Rashid's stare seemed unfocused and distant, even though he was looking directly at Caine.

"You kidnapped this mother's two sons when you attacked her Bedouin camp. At least tell her their fate."

Safiya gasped, then quickly brought her emotions under control. Kimberly gripped her hand. The two women hung their heads, not wishing to make eye contact with the uncaring, monstrous man who stood before them.

"Very well." Rashid made a signal to his men that it was time to move out. "Al Qaeda has them. Those that survive Khaldun's brutal training will become his new recruits. She can pray to Allah that death, a far kinder fate, awaits her sons."

"You're making deals with Ahmed Khaldun now? An Al Qaeda regional commander?" Caine asked. He had heard of this particular Yemeni terrorist. Khaldun was an explosives expert, with a knack for evading American surveillance. He had escaped many attempts to hunt him down.

"Don't be naïve, Caine," Rashid replied. "We all make deals with the devil when it suits our purpose. Remember your history. The United States backed Saddam Hussein in the Iran-Iraq War in the eighties. Then they turned against him and invaded his country in the two Gulf Wars."

Rashid walked back to his Humvee while his men kept Caine, Safiya and Kimberley in their sights. Then returned to their respective armored vehicles, and drove off into the desert.

When they were far from sight, Caine stood, gritting his teeth hard. He had been betrayed, set up not only by the Saudis, but by Forster. A man he had never met. A man who was using Caine for his own unscrupulous ends, and who had betrayed his own lover, Emily Argyle. A man who had sent her to her death.

But those were all moot points now. They had no water, no weapons, food, transport or means of communications. They might last through the day and the night if they were lucky. But after that, thirst would kill them.

"What do we do now?" Kimberley asked hopefully.

Caine was about to answer, when Safiya spoke.

"There is something I didn't tell either of you. If Allah is willing, something that might save us all!"

CHAPTER TWENTY-ONE

"One of the passengers walked from the crash," Safiya explained. "He still died after he bled to death. But he managed to walk to a small rock formation, west of here."

Caine looked at her, surprised. "Why are you only telling us this now?"

"I needed to hold something back, just in case you wouldn't help me find my children. Information I could bargain with. But now... I saw what you did. You tricked that soldier into telling you where my children are. I... I thank you."

Caine glared at her, not sure how he should react to this revelation.

"If you're having a go at Safiya for holding back information, just look in the mirror," Kimberley interrupted. "How long did it take you to tell us your real name?"

"Okay," Caine said quietly. "Safiya and I both haven't been completely honest here. I get that, and we each had our reasons. But right now, we need to find a way out of our situation here, or we'll be dead within the next forty-eight hours."

He could feel the sweat running off him. The dry heat had to be

126

more than a hundred degrees, and there was no shade. Without water, they wouldn't last long.

"Do either of you have water on you?" he asked.

The two women shook their heads.

"What about the camels?" Kimberley asked. "Could we survive eating camel meat?"

"They were burnt to cinders, there's nothing left but ash. Plus I'm pretty sure the chemicals in Hellfire missiles would be toxic." Caine turned to Safiya. "Who was this man? The one who walked away from the crash?"

Safiya shook her head. "I don't know who he was. He was dark skinned, like an African man."

Caine considered this information. Jarod Forster was African-American. But according to Rashid, Forster was still alive. He wasn't on the plane when it went down...

Safiya continued speaking, her voice dry and hoarse. "He managed to walk from the wreckage. I saw his body huddled in some rocks, but before I could reach him the sandstorm hit."

Caine thought for a moment. "So his body might still be there, with provisions, weapons and a means of communication?"

The Bedouin woman gave him a confused look, then shrugged. "Maybe... I do not know."

"Can you take us there?"

She nodded. "I think so."

They climbed a dune. Together they scanned the western horizon. Eventually Kimberley spotted the rocky embankment, jutting up from the sand. Caine guessed it was perhaps three, maybe four miles distant.

They took off at a brisk pace, walking along the tops of the dunes as much as they could so they didn't lose sight of the rock. Caine's tongue felt thick and swollen. He was thirsty, desperate for a drink. He pushed those thoughts aside and kept marching. Caine knew the man Safiya had seen, whoever he was, might be their only hope. But first they had to find him. He would either have water on him... or he would not. When all their problems were broken down into their component pieces, it was that simple. Fix one thing at a time, then move onto the next.

Caine glanced at the two women marching alongside him. To Safiya and Kimberley's credit, they kept pace with him, and never complained once. He knew that they too must be desperate to quench their thirst.

Walking was not easy. The sand was soft and treacherous, especially when they needed to climb a dune. A journey that would have taken an hour on solid ground took three through the shifting desert.

When they reached the rock outcropping, Caine could see it was about six-hundred feet long, thirty feet wide and about twenty feet high. The rocks themselves resembled dried honeycombs. Dead grass grew in clumps around the base of the steep sandstone edges. Caine saw no signs of the corpse. Whatever tracks the man had left would have been blown away by the winds long ago.

"Where did you see him?" Caine demanded of Safiya. "Which crevasse?"

Safiya shook her head. "I don't remember."

"Try," he insisted. Caine knew he was pushing her, but the alternatives weren't pretty for any of them. He was already becoming light headed from thirst. "The body will be buried. There are only so many times we can dig before we lose our strength. We have to narrow our search."

She nodded, finding her courage. "Let me take a closer look."

As he examined the rocks, Caine identified petroglyphs on their jagged faces. The stylized carvings depicted men, camels and oryx. They could have been thousands of years old, for all Caine knew.

Safiya examined each rock face with him, searching for anything familiar. Caine could see she was having a hard time. Too much had changed since the passing of two sandstorms. He scanned the rocks with a critical eye. He tried to guess where he would have hidden, if he were the one alone in the desert, bleeding to death.

He quickly identified three possible locations, and pointed them out to the women.

"Alright, we'd better get started, Kimberly and Safiya, you take those two sections over there. I'll start at those rocks in the middle."

The two women nodded, and they split up. They each began scooping into the mounds of sand that had blown up against the rock faces. They had only their hands to work with, and the labor was exhausting under the brutal sun. He lost track of how long he'd been digging. Was it a few minutes... an hour? More?

Suddenly, he heard Kimberley call out.

"Thomas!"

"What did you find?"

"A locket."

Safiya and Caine ran to Kimberley. She had discovered a locket hanging from the rock. He opened it, and found a tiny, faded photograph inside. It was a picture of Emily Argyle and Jarod Forster, together. They looked happy and in love.

"What does that mean?" Kimberley asked.

Caine again felt a sense of uncertainty. "This man was one of the crew, Jarod Forster. He was supposedly in love with my friend, Emily Argyle. This is them."

"That's so romantic," Kimberley said as she examined the locket in Caine's hand. "He saved this locket from the crash. His last thoughts were of her."

Kimberley explored the rocks near where she had found the locket. "There might be something else here." She pulled aside several loose rock fragments. They tumbled and fell on the ledge beneath her.

CRACK! CRACK!

The sound of gunfire echoed around them. Caine and Kimberly ducked behind the rocks. He peered around the side, looking for an attacker, but there was no one.

Kimberly opened her eyes and straightened from the hunched position she had adopted. She too looked for the shooter.

Safiya, unperturbed, grabbed another rock and smashed it on the rock edge. Another loud crack rang out. It sounded like a gunshot.

"It's okay," she called out. "It's just the rocks!"

"Wow!" Kimberley said in awe. "I thought we were dead, but it's just the acoustics in here. The echo makes it sound like gunshots."

"Some of the rocks in the desert are very old," Safiya explained. "They can carry whispers for great distances. If you know where to speak to them."

Caine nodded, relieved that they weren't under attack. "Kimberley, did you find anything else behind the rocks you pulled down?"

She shook her head. "Sorry, got a bit optimistic there."

He stared at the locket again. For a moment, Caine was jealous of Jarod Forster and Emily Argyle's relationship. The way they held each other in the photo... He had never expressed commitment or devotion to Rebecca Freeling like that. He didn't know if he ever could.

Had Rashid got it wrong? A man who hangs a locket expressing his eternal love, while bleeding out in the heart of a wasteland... Was that the kind of man to set up his girlfriend to take a fall?

He snapped the locket closed. The mystery would have to wait.

"Let's keep digging," he said. "See if we can find anything useful."

They worked together, pushing aside the hot sands. They first had to use their head scarves so the sand wouldn't burn their hands. But a foot down the sand was much cooler. After thirty minutes or so of frantic shoveling, Kimberley let out a tiny squeal of excitement. Then she kept digging. A mummified husk of a hand, then a limb, and finally a whole body was unearthed.

The clothes were western. Cotton shirt and pants, desert boots, and a worn leather belt. Multiple lacerations cut across the body, probably where fragments of the plane's wreckage had cut or impaled him. The sunken face and shriveled skin robbed the man of any identifying features. But Caine was certain this was Jarod Forster. His wallet held an Arizona driver's license and social security card with his name on them. The passport stuffed in his pocket further confirmed his identity.

Sulieman Rashid was either wrong, or lying. Whoever he was dealing with inside the CIA, it was not Jarod Forster.

Caine kept searching. He flipped open the man's shirt pocket. Inside, his probing fingers wrapped around a slim metal rectangle.

The data stick, he thought. The item which had started him on this cross-global investigation in the first place. The secret Emily, Forster, and so many others had died for.

He discretely pocketed the stick without the women noticing. He kept digging. Kimberley and Safiya helped. Soon they found a Browning Hi-Power pistol, a half-full water bottle, and a satellite phone.

"If he had water, why didn't he drink it?" Kimberley asked.

"Perhaps his wounds made it too painful to drink," Safiya offered. "Or he might have finished other water bottles first, dropping them when they were empty."

They rationed out the water. Each of them drank a sixth now, saving the rest for later. Caine entrusted Safiya to hold the water bottle.

Kimberly licked her lips, hungry for every last drop of the precious liquid. "While I'm asking all the questions, why didn't Forster call for help on the sat phone?"

Caine examined it. The answer was obvious. "Because the battery was missing," he said.

A thought occurred to him. Caine took the battery from his pocket and tried it on Forster's phone. To his surprise, it fit. Both phones were the same make and model.

"Looks like we finally got a break," Caine muttered. The phone switched on. The screen lit up and locked in on a signal, providing them with the GPS coordinates for their position.

"Who do we call?" Kimberley asked. "Who can get here fast enough?"

Caine knew exactly who he needed to speak to.

He dialed the number from memory. Gabriella Castro answered after three rings.

Caine quickly explained their circumstances. In short, clipped sentences, he told her that he knew where the missing data stick was, that they needed immediate evacuation.

He took a breath after finishing his story. "Who's in charge now that Delbridge has been taken out?" he finally asked.

"What?" Gabriella responded, surprise evident in her tone. "Martin Delbridge isn't dead... He's right here. He's on the other line, listening to this conversation."

Caine froze. His fist tightened around the phone, clenching it in a white knuckled grip. "What?"

"Do you want to speak to him?"

Caine terminated the call quickly, but he knew it was already too late. Their location was in the hands of the enemy, and that enemy was Martin Delbridge. The CIA Station Head was the man in collusion with Rashid. He was pretending to be Forster whenever they spoke.

Caine remembered the program Gabriella had shown him, Mustang Sally. Delbridge must have used it to mask his identity, in case Rashid cracked his communication encryptions. And Delbridge had faked his death in Sana'a to scare Caine into working alone. No wonder the van had snatched his body away so quickly...

Anger welled up inside Caine, but he bit it down. He knew he had to remain cool and calm. Survival was their first priority. They had to escape this desert. Then he could go after Martin Delbridge, and take him down.

"Why did you hang up?" Safiya asked.

Kimberly looked into his smoldering green eyes. "What the hell is going on?" she demanded.

"We've been set up," Caine answered. "Either that drone is going to come back and finish us off, or Rashid and his men are."

CHAPTER TWENTY-TWO

A look of panic flashed across both women's faces.

"They have to find us first," Caine responded calmly. "It's been about four hours since Rashid's men left us. Let's assume it will take them that long to find us again."

Caine dialed a second number into the phone. The secure line required him to code in with an eight digit alpha-numeric password. There was a brief click after his identity was confirmed.

Rebecca Freeling picked up even faster than Gabriella had.

"Tom?" she answered hesitantly.

"Yeah, it's me."

"I can hear that. Where the hell are you?"

He gave her their GPS coordinates.

"That's in the middle of the Arabian desert."

"Yeah. No time to explain. How quickly can you get an evac team to this position? There's three of us, including me."

"Wait a second." He could hear her tapping away at a keyboard. "I can get an Osprey Tiltrotor with long range fuel tanks out of Camp Lemonnier, Djibouti. They can reach you in about four hours, and there's a Delta Force team onboard."

"That's cutting it close."

"What do you mean?" He could hear the concern in her voice. "Close to what?"

"The Saudi Army is coming for us. ETA four hours. That's assuming a drone doesn't pick us up first."

More keyboard tapping. "We have another problem, Tom. Something you've overlooked." Her voice sounded scared, even frantic. Caine didn't like the sound of it.

"More good news," he muttered. "What is it now?"

"You're in Saudi airspace. I can't send a military team in there, not without provoking a major diplomatic incident."

Caine gritted his teeth. He couldn't believe they were about to be abandoned because of a legal technicality.

"Tom, can you get to Yemen?"

"No chance. We have no transport."

The line became silent, although he could still hear her breathing.

"Tom?"

He sensed she wanted to tell him something. Something important. He thought about the picture in the locket, Emily and Jarod. The longing in their eyes. The emptiness he felt...

"Rebecca? I..." His voice trailed off.

He remembered the last time he had seen her... the hotel in Australia. And before that, the briefing in the airport. Her beaming smile, as she revealed her intel on the operation Emily and Jarod were part of.

A joint operation, with the Saudis...

"Wait a second," he said, remembering what he had learned about the U.S.-Saudi operation so far. "Try the code SANDFIRE with the Saudis. The CIA transport route you told me about. They're in on it, so they should authorize the flight, so long as you tell them it's transporting goods."

"Okay, hold on. This might take me a few minutes."

"Thanks Rebecca. Awaiting your instructions."

Mentally he kicked himself. She had been able to tell him how she really felt about him, but the moment had been lost. He found himself wanting her to tell him, rather than leave their relationship in a state of limbo all the time. He looked at Kimberley looking back at him, sadness in her stare. She had guessed from his expression this was the women who had captured Caine's heart. He didn't know what to say, so he said nothing.

Eight minutes passed before Rebecca spoke again. "My superiors want to know if you have the data stick, with the compromising information on it?"

Caine gritted his teeth. He thought about his promise to Safiya.

"No," he lied, "but I know where it is."

"Tom, I need to know now. Where is it?"

Caine knew he was gambling with his own life and the lives of the two women with him. Not to mention the lives of several dozen children. He needed the data stick to leverage the children's rescue.

"Okay Rebecca, I've got the coordinates. They are—," he began. Then he removed the battery from the phone, killing the call in a brief blip of static.

He looked up at the two women. Safiya and Kimberley were staring at him in disbelief.

"Trust me," he said. "I know what I'm doing."

"Are we being rescued?" Kimberley asked.

"Are you still going to save my sons?" Safiya added.

"Yes, to both your questions. But it's complicated. In four hours, we'll either be tackling U.S. drones, the Saudi Army, or both. A covert extraction team is on its way to rescue us. We need to be prepared. We have to survive until then."

Kimberly glared at him as if he was crazy. "I like your optimism, but how do you propose we do that?"

Caine began to formulate a plan in his mind. Against the drone they had no chance. But he was betting it would be Rashid and his men who returned. The Colonel would want to ensure Caine wasn't lying about the data stick. After all the trouble it had caused, Rashid would want to see it with his own eyes, before he destroyed it once and for all.

The only chance they had against three heavily armed Humvees was to lay in ambush, and hope to take one by force. It wasn't good odds, but it was better than no odds.

He explained the plan and then they got to work.

Caine stripped from his Bedouin clothes. Soon, he was dressed only in his white cotton shirt, khaki cargo pants and desert boots. The two women used his discarded clothes to make a dummy in the shape of a man, lying supine in the desert sands. They stuffed the empty clothes with rocks and sand to give them a human shape.

Next, they dug a hole for Caine to hide in, where he would be armed with the Browning Hi-Power. He cleaned the pistol as best he could, despite the lack of oil or other lubricants to do the job. The arid conditions had worked in the gun's favor, and it seemed to operate fine. He tested it by firing a single bullet into a dune.

Kimberley, meanwhile, removed her Abaya. Underneath she wore a tank top and loose cotton pants. Caine realized this was the first time he had seen her without the fabric covering her body. She was tall and slim, and very attractive. Her fair skin would burn quickly in the hot sun, but that was the least of their problems.

When their preparations were complete, they drank the last of their water. Then Safiya and Kimberley buried Caine under the Abaya. They left an opening in the sand, just wide enough for him to peer out towards the dummy on the rocks.

He watched them climb up onto the rocky outcrop until they reached the top. They hid inside the crevasse. They had tested for ideal positions earlier, and were ready with their distraction.

While he waited, Caine again checked the Browning Hi-Power pistol. He had twelve rounds of the 9×19mm Parabellum bullets left in the thirteen round magazine.

He was up against twelve highly trained and battle hardened soldiers of the Saudi Army. He knew had to make every shot count.

CHAPTER TWENTY-THREE

Rashid and his three Humvees showed up an hour before sunset, churning sand as they plowed through the dunes. They didn't bother with stealth. They had superior numbers and firepower, and they knew it.

Silent and still, Caine watched from his foxhole. Three soldiers climbed out of the first Humvee. Within seconds, they peppered the fake corpse on the rocks with a barrage of gunfire from their assault rifles.

That was Kimberley and Safiya's signal. Hidden in the crevasse, they smashed rocks against the shear wall opposite them.

CRACK! CRACK!

Once again, the strange acoustics of the crevasse amplified the noise, make the crashing rocks sound like rifle shots. The cacophony was enough to distract the soldiers. The startled men spun around, and opened fire on the rock walls.

As the men turned their backs on him, Caine took aim with the Browning. He lined up the closest soldier and shot him in the back of the head, just as the man finished reloading his weapon.

Flinging away his sand covered hideout, he sprinted to the fallen corpse. In a single fluid motion, he lifted the man's rifle, pulled back on the charging handle, and squeezed the progressive trigger. A full automatic burst sprayed from the rifle, striking the two other soldiers from the Humvee.

Within seconds, Caine grabbed a spare magazine from the downed men, and ran to the Humvee. So far, no one inside the vehicle had seen him. Thanks to the women's distraction, the soldier in the turret was busy firing at the rock outcropping. Caine ejected the translucent empty magazine, and reloaded his rifle. Then he threw open the back door of the truck.

Caine fired again, tearing open the meat on the gunner's legs. He adjusted his aim, and a stream of bullets punctured the driver's head and throat multiple times.

Caine dropped the rifle and pulled his pistol from his waistband. He leapt inside the vehicle and shot the howling gunner in the chest, before the man could climb back into the Humvee.

Less than thirty seconds had elapsed... enough time for the remaining soldiers to notice his ambush. Caine pushed the driver's corpse out the door, then slid behind the wheel.

Two ground soldiers opened fire on Caine's position, their Steyrs in full automatic mode. Gunfire peppered his Humvee's windshield with cracks and holes until it shattered. Caine ducked low and floored the accelerator. The massive vehicle charged forward, roaring towards his attackers. Seconds later, two thumps beneath the Humvee told him his assailants had been taken out.

Seven down. Five to go.

Caine sat up, and assessed his situation. The two remaining Humvees were in sight, about three-hundred yards distant. They were parked at the base of a sand dune, below him now. Much to Caine's dismay, one was armed with a belt feed grenade launcher. The heavy weapon roared, spitting a barrage of 40mm high explosive grenades in his direction.

Caine slammed down on the gas pedal and turned, but he couldn't accelerate fast enough. Grenades exploded around him, shattering the remaining glass and cutting him multiple times. Sand filled the air, forcing him to cough and gag.

He didn't see the grenade that hit. But he felt its explosive impact shake the vehicle.

A geyser of sand erupted beneath him. The Humvee flipped over and launched into the air. Caine barely managed to slip his arm into the seatbelt. The thin fabric strap was all he had to stop himself from being thrown around the cabin, or flung from the vehicle.

The Humvee collided with the sand. A jarring thud reverberated through Caine's body. Every bone in his body felt as if it had been flexed to the breaking point, and he groaned with staggering pain.

But it wasn't over yet.

Now he was spinning, tumbling over and over in circles. He realized his vehicle was rolling down the side of a dune.

He could do nothing, so he hung on for his life. He tried to count how many times he turned, but he could never tell which way was up. Sand filled the cabin getting in his mouth, nostrils and eyes. The noise of grinding metal assaulted his ears. The shocks to his body felt like a pummeling from multiple opponents.

Finally, the rolling slowed. The battered vehicle's chassis tilted, then stopped all together.

Caine opened his eyes. He spat out a mouthful of sand, and cursed the pain wracking every part of his anatomy. He realized he was alive, and to his immense surprise only superficially injured.

He was also upright, facing one of the other vehicles. The heavy truck's side was turned towards him.

It was the Humvee with the grenade launcher, and it was too close to fire on him. At this range, the explosive projectiles would take out both vehicles.

To Caine's surprise, Sulieman Rashid stared back at him from the passenger window. His expression was blank, probably wondering how Caine had survived.

Caine didn't think or hesitate. He fired the ignition and floored the accelerator. The engine roared to life. His vehicle lurched forward, ramming into the passenger side of Rashid's Humvee.

The impact catapulted Caine forward. The seatbelt wrapped around his left arm stopped him from hurtling through the shattered windscreen.

The second Humvee fared much worse from the collision. The impact knocked it on its side, leaving the undercarriage facing towards Caine.

Stumbling, disoriented and wracked with pain, Caine pushed through the hurt. Blood dribbled down the side of his head. He gritted his teeth as he pulled a long shard of glass out of his left shoulder. Then he grabbed another Steyr assault rifle from the passenger seat.

When he stepped onto the sand he almost fell. His head spun and his eyes couldn't focus. His left knee felt like it had been taken to with a hammer. Putting weight on it was manageable, but agonizing.

Steyr out in front, he advanced around the rolled Humvee. He used the battered truck as cover from the last Humvee, which was now accelerating towards him.

Caine heard movement, scurrying from the overturned truck. He spun around, just as a soldier climbed from the side of the overturned vehicle.

Caine fired a single shot, and put a bullet in his heart.

The final Humvee was almost upon him. It kicked up a cloud of sand as it raced towards his position, its engine snarling like a hungry tiger.

Ducking back behind the rolled truck, Caine lifted his Steyr rifle. He stared down the back circle in the scope until he lined up the driver. He squeezed down on the trigger, nearly emptying the magazine.

The opposing vehicle's windshield shattered, and the Humvee turned in a wide circle. He heard the brakes squeal, as the truck struggled to control its frantic skid. Caine lined up the driver again and fired. His bullets found their mark, killing the man instantly.

Dropping the empty rifle, Caine drew his Browning pistol. He limped to a better position to observe the last Humvee.

The gunner was trying to unjam the mounted .50 caliber belt-fed machine gun.

Caine aimed his pistol and put a bullet into the man's mouth. The projectile must have ricocheted off the back of the soldier's helmet... the soldier's face exploded outwards in a shower of wet meat.

Eleven dead. That only left Rashid to deal with.

Caine picked up another discarded Steyr, along with an ammo vest holding multiple magazines. He set off, looking for the Colonel. The military intelligence officer was nowhere to be seen. A few yards away, Caine found footsteps in the sand leading up the side of a dune.

He tried jogging but his knee hurt too much. He limped instead, putting most of his weight on his right leg as he advanced up the hillside.

When he crossed the top, he saw no sign of Rashid. Kimberley lay sprawled in the sand, crying in pain. A wet patch of red spread from her abdomen.

Safiya knelt over her, pressing her hand against the wound, trying to slow the bleeding. She looked up when she saw Caine. Her eyes grew wide in fear as she called out. "Thomas! Behind you."

Caine didn't have time to turn. He felt a powerful force ram into the back of his head. He stumbled, dropped the Steyr and spun around. Rashid rushed him again, fists swinging. The bigger man punched him in the face.

Caine stumbled again and teetered backwards. He realized he was about to tumble weaponless down the side of a dune. His arm shot out, grabbed Rashid by the shirt, and yanked him forward.

They both fell, rolling a hundred feet down the side of the dune.

When they slammed into the bottom, Caine staggered to his feet. He shuffled forward, feeling drunk from the battering he had taken.

Rashid came at him. His powerful fists jabbed at Caine's gut, chest and arms. The man's bulging arms were like rods of steel. Caine could barely hold himself upright, as the Colonel's onslaught battered him backwards.

Then something switched inside Caine. He pushed through the pain and disorientation. He let instinct and muscle memory guide him. Rashid's unnaturally powerful jabs shot towards him again. This time, Caine was ready with blocks and deflections. Rashid continued his unrelenting rain of blows. The beast of a man outweighed Caine by fifty pounds or more of pure muscle. He was like an accelerating freight train, battering a car stranded on the tracks. He had no fear, and nothing held him back.

Caine blocked again and again, but he still took a beating. With a sinking feeling in his gut, he realized he was losing. He was up against a foe of superior skill and strength. How much longer could he last? A minute? Two at the most?

Suddenly, both men were engulfed by a deafening roar. Sand lifted and spun around them in swirling gusts. Rashid's head jerked up in surprise as the Osprey Tiltrotor descended towards them. Caine avoided the temptation to follow his gaze.

This is my chance, he thought.

He took advantage of the opening in Rashid's guard. He ran at his foe, swinging his right fist out in a powerful jab of his own. His knuckles rammed into Rashid's throat.

The Colonel didn't see it coming. He staggered backwards, gasping for breath and clutching his crushed windpipe. Rashid fell to his knees. A hoarse groan wheezed from his gaping mouth.

Caine saw dark shapes dropping towards him through the whirling sand. He looked left and right... He found himself surrounded by black uniformed soldiers. The men's uniforms carried no insignia or markings, and each soldier carried an M4 carbine. Tactical PICO plate carriers with ammo pouches, and holstered MARSOC M45 Close Quarter Battle Pistols completed their equipment load.

Delta Force operators, Caine thought. The U.S. Army's most elite Special Forces soldiers.

"Thomas Caine, I presume?" said an operator who rushed up beside him. The man's M4 drew a bead on the wounded Rashid. "Let me introduce myself. Sergeant Jack Tyler, 1st Special Forces Operational Detachment-Delta. I hear you and two civilians need an air lift?"

Catching his breath, Caine nodded. "Appreciate the assist, Sergeant. I have a wounded civilian up there." He pointed up the rise of the dune he'd tumbled down. "She needs immediate evac."

"What about this one?" Tyler pointed to Rashid. The Saudi officer was still panting, gasping for breath.

"We need to take him in. He can tell us exactly where Al Qaeda's Regional Commander Ahmed Khaldun is hiding."

"And the location of the missing data stick?"

Caine touched the data stick in his pocket, grateful he hadn't lost it during the bloody battle. "Yeah. Khaldun has it. We find Khaldun, we find the data stick."

In a rapid, fluid motion, Rashid pulled a knife from a sheath hidden in his shirt sleeve. Before Caine and Tyler could move, he impaled the blade deep into his throat. Blood gushed like a fountain, and he fell forward. He was dead before his face struck the sand.

Caine rolled the corpse over. The man's eyes were wide open, and stared forward. His expression was blank and unreadable. He was the same in death as he had been in life... an empty shell, devoid of all emotion.

"Well fuck!" exclaimed Tyler. "That's not something you see every day!"

CHAPTER TWENTY-FOUR

AL JAWF GOVERNORATE, YEMEN

The Osprey Tiltrotor flew fast and low over the desert. Its airframe shook and rattled against the buffeting winds, as it pushed its velocity to maximum speed. They crossed into Yemeni airspace long before Saudi Arabian F-15 jet fighters could move to intercept. Caine guessed that a diplomatic incident could soon be on the table. He hoped the compromising data he carried in his pocket would change all that.

His immediate concern was Kimberley. She lay panting on a stretcher. The knife wound Rashid had inflicted was deep. The medic had controlled the bleeding, then hooked her up to IV fluids, but that was all he could do. Sergeant Tyler was a universal donor, he was supplying his own blood to Kimberley. They were keeping her alive, but just barely.

"How's she doing," Caine asked, keeping his voice as low as he could in the loud aircraft's interior.

The medic glanced down at Kimberly from the corner of his eyes, making sure she wasn't watching. Then he shook his head.

Caine knew what that meant. Only surgery could save her now. That meant reaching Djibouti as soon as possible.

"Tom?" She reached out and Caine grabbed her hand. She was using the shortened version of his name... like Rebecca did. Her grip was tight but her eyes were unfocused.

"I'm here, Kimberley."

"How... how bad is it?"

He had seen the wound. There was a good chance it had punctured a kidney or her liver. The gash itself was at least four inches long.

"It's not that bad. You're going to be fine."

She turned her head, focused on Caine. "You sure? Because it bloody hurts." She coughed, and fresh blood spattered her shirt. Her body contorted with pain.

The medic stepped in, pushing Caine aside. The skin glue he had applied had come undone, and she was bleeding again.

Caine stepped back. He leaned against the fuselage, and felt the rattling of the Tiltrotor jarring his sore bones. They sped on into the night. Safiya sat next to him, sobbing quietly. Caine knew why.

"Thomas, I'm so sorry about Kimberley. I told her not to come down from the rock, but she insisted."

"She's going to be fine," Caine lied again. "Look, I know why you're upset, Safiya. I haven't forgotten my promise. As soon as we get the intel we need, I'll personally lead the team to kill the bastard. We'll get your sons back."

Caine was angry with himself for dropping his guard long enough for Rashid to take his own life. The one link to the Bedouin children's location, snatched away from him in an instant.

He had already lied to Kimberley about her chances of survival. Now he was lying to Safiya about her chances of finding Mohammad and Hussein. As soon as Khaldun heard of Rashid's demise, he would move his army of terrorists to a new location.

Caine felt for the data stick in his pocket again. He hated lying to Rebecca, and these men, and he wondered if he should reveal that he had it on him. But to do so would be to give up on his promise to Safiya.

The Bedouin mother leaned close, and whispered in his ear. "You have it don't you... this data stick that everyone wants?"

He stared at her, confused. "How did you know?" he asked in equally hushed tones.

"You keep touching it," she whispered again. "I've seen you looking at it when you think no one is watching. Why haven't you told anyone about it?"

Caine grimaced. His wounds had been treated, yet his body still ached all over. But he was determined to remain combat ready. He'd even kitted up, with body armor, a tactical vest, and a MARSOC M45 Close Quarter Battle Pistol in a belt holster. If he needed an M4 carbine, all he had to do was ask and it would be provided to him. His mission here was far from complete.

"Thomas?"

He leaned closer to her. "Keep your voice down. You heard Rashid... Khaldun has your children. And if the CIA know I have the stick, they have no reason to hunt down Khaldun. He's not that big in the scheme of global terrorism."

"Khaldun? But I already know where he is."

"You do?" Caine asked with surprise.

She nodded.

"Where?"

"The mountains north of Al Abr. He leads the Al Qaeda group we have to pay for their 'protection' services."

"Could you find it on a map?"

She nodded.

Caine stared at her for a long few seconds while a plan formulated, one he knew could work. But there was one serious problem.

"Kimberley?" He turned and grabbed the young Australian woman's hand again.

She barely noticed him. "Tom!" she said half delirious. "That name suits you. Better... better than Matthew... or even Thomas."

"Kimberley, listen to me."

She smiled for him, looking like a drunk. "I'm listening Tom. We have to save... the children."

"We need to get you to a hospital first."

"No. No you don't. We... we made a promise, remember?"

"Yes, I know."

"We both did... so you better keep it."

Her hand became limp, and slipped away.

"Is she...?" Caine asked, afraid what the answer might be.

The medic checked her pulse and breathing. Shook his head. "No, she's with us, but she's weak."

Kimberley had slipped into unconsciousness and that was not a good sign. Her only chance was trauma surgery at Camp Lemonnier, still a few hours away.

Grabbing a map from Tyler, Caine instructed Safiya to show him exactly where the Al Qaeda hideout was. She was very precise with her directions so Caine felt confident the risk was worth taking. He quickly assessed it would be a forty-minute diversion from their original flight path.

"It's nightfall," Caine said, finding a pair of night vision goggles and slipping them on over his head, ready to flip down when he needed them. "Sergeant, you drop me here," —he pointed to a location several hundred feet from the supposed Al Qaeda camp— "then high tail it back to Djibouti."

"How will you get out again?" Tyler asked.

"There are trucks in the camp. Safiya said Khaldun owns several. Plus, if I'm going to get the children out while I find that data stick, I'll need something to drive them out in."

"You won't get three dozen kids in one truck."

Caine shrugged, knowing that he didn't have an answer for that one, but determined to go anyway.

"I'll come with you," Safiya offered. The two men stared at her, silently questioning her sanity. "I am nothing without Mohammad and Hussein," she replied. "My life will mean nothing if they die. If I must give my life to save them, then may Allah give me the strength to do so."

"Fine," Caine responded, before he could change his mind. "We'll get you body armor, comms, and a pistol. But you stay out of sight until I'm done."

"I think you mean 'We're done'," Tyler said with a grin.

"We?"

"You think I'm gonna miss out on a chance to kill a bunch of terrorist assholes? I'd never live it down if I didn't come."

Caine grinned back, pleased with how this was turning out. "Most appreciated Sergeant."

Tyler looked him in the eyes. "Don't mention it. These guys are holding a bunch of kids hostage. And there's some things a man just can't abide. Know what I mean?"

Caine nodded. "I do."

In hushed tones, he began to outline a rescue plan.

CHAPTER TWENTY-FIVE

The Osprey Tiltrotor lowered its rear loading ramp, letting the buffeting winds sweep through the interior. While the gunner let loose a volley of tracer rounds with his M240 machine gun, Tyler, with Safiya strapped to his harness, rappelled to the ground. Caine followed close behind. They hit the rocky surface in less than five seconds, detached the ropes and sprinted for cover. It was dark, and Caine didn't think they'd been spotted.

No one's shooting at us, he thought.

The Tiltrotor hovered above. The gunner fired again, and dropped a few grenades. The aircraft swooped over the area, repeating the process a couple more times at different locations. Gunfire streaked up from the shadowed rocks, pelting the side of the Tiltrotor. When the aircraft finally sustained damage, it lifted and flew east. The crew had done what had been asked of them. They had rattled the cage. The Taliban rats had emerged from their caves, furious and eager to retaliate.

Caine and Tyler watched the carnage unfold through their night vision goggles. The Taliban had taken significant casualties from the Osprey's assault.

"Perfect distraction," Tyler whispered.

Caine nodded. "Hopefully they'll be too busy searching for the Osprey to see us coming."

"You wait here," Caine instructed Safiya. "If you see the trucks drive out with the children, meet us on the road down there." He pointed towards the trail that led out of the rugged terrain. "If we're not back in two hours, get as far away as you can. You know where to go?"

She nodded. "There is a village nearby where I have family. My sister."

"Good, then we'll be off."

"Good luck. And Thomas... Allah praise you for what you have done."

He put his hand on her shoulder. "This nightmare will all be over soon, Safiya, I promise."

Then he and Tyler turned, and disappeared into the shadows between the rocks.

———

Tyler and Caine descended down the side of the mountain, taking quick, quiet steps. Their M4 assault rifles were fitted with silencers. Shooting would attract minimal attention. Failing that, their twelve-inch carbon steel-bladed tactical knives and .45 ACP semi-automatic pistols could do the job just as well.

The first insurgents they encountered didn't see them coming. They were too busy making shrill noises and waving their AK-47s in the air. Caine and Tyler paused and aimed with their rifles. Double tap shots silenced them quickly.

As the men struck the ground, another Al Qaeda fighter caught a glimpse of them from the corner of his eye. He spun around, firing off a burst from his AK. His shots went wide and missed them completely. Tyler didn't even stop moving as he put two bullets into the man's chest, then another into his twitching corpse.

No one else came to investigate. The other insurgents were too busy shooting into the skies, trying to take out the Tiltrotor that was long gone.

"What does this Khaldun look like again?" Tyler asked. "Ugly, I bet."

"Very," Caine replied softly over the mic. "Left side of his face is burned by an IED that went off too soon. He's hard to miss."

"Roger that."

As they drew closer to the center of the base, they saw more insurgents darting through the shadows. But with the help of the night vision goggles, they were able to move silently through the darkness. No one saw Caine and Tyler coming. Their rifles barked quiet death as they made their way past the men. A dozen terrorists were silenced permanently, and without anyone noticing.

Eventually they came upon the main section of the camp. The towering rocks were lit up by flickering camp fires. Men in thoobs and turbans proudly carried their AK-47s, and displayed their Janbiya knives in belt sheaths. Caine counted twenty-two. Tyler repeated the same count. The Taliban seemed to be regrouping now that they realized the Osprey was gone.

"Two o'clock." Caine whispered the direction. "Two ridged cattle trucks."

"I see them," Tyler said, as his eyes locked on the pair of vehicles.

"Two should be enough to drive out the kids." Caine reloaded his rifle with a fresh magazine.

"If we can find them."

"We'll find them," Caine said firmly. "But we need Khaldun first, for the data stick."

"That must be him." Tyler pointed out an elderly man with horrific scars on his face, exactly as Caine had described. The man's cheeks looked sunken and collapsed. He had lost muscle mass as well as skin. In profile, Khaldun resembled a desiccated corpse. He pointed and gestured wildly, and appeared to be arguing with a squad of his men.

"Whew... definitely not his good side," Tyler whispered. "Lot's of targets between him and us. We'll need to take them out first."

"Roger that."

Caine scanned the small valley in detail. There was a single road exiting the mountains, which would be how they would drive out. Caine also noticed water channels cutting through the rocks. They were designed to flow downhill, branching off into multiple paths. All but one of the junctions had stones in them to stop the flow of water. These channels no doubt led to villages lower down the mountains.

That's one way Khaldun's Al Qaeda cell makes their money, Caine thought. *They take bribes to release the water for the communities downstream.*

Caine traced the channel up the side of the hill, where it disappeared into the dark rocks. He knew many settlements in the Middle East had extensive water tunnels like these. They were constructed in mountains and deserts to control the flow of water from rain catchment areas into the more arid regions. These tunnels might be hundreds of years old. They could extend for hundreds of miles, and there would be no light down there.

Caine and Tyler watched for a few minutes, guns aimed down at the insurgents. They waited for an opportunity.

Eventually it came, but Caine didn't like it. Khaldun concluded his heated discussion with his men, and disappeared inside the water tunnel.

"You see that?" Caine asked.

"Khaldun going to the mountain? Guess Mohammad isn't coming to him."

"I'm going after him. You set up a series of explosive charges like we planned. When I return, blow them to cover our escape. And remember, I won't be coming out alone."

"What makes you think the kids are in there?" Tyler hissed back.

"I don't see anywhere else they could be hidden. They have to be in there somewhere."

Tyler glanced over at him. A bead of sweat ran down his face. "You sure about this? Going in there alone?"

Caine kept his eyes on the camp below. "I made a promise. I intend to keep it."

"Two pairs of eyes are better than one. Let me—"

Caine shook his head. "I need you out here. Stick to the plan. Give me one hour. If I'm not out by then, find Safiya and get away from here."

"Roger that. And Caine... good hunting!"

Caine sidestepped down the steep, rocky hill, then kept to the shadows as he approached the tunnel. No one guarded where the channel poured water from the mountain, so he walked straight into it. Ten feet in, the water rose up to his knees. He placed the data stick in a waterproof pouch provided to him on the Osprey, and sealed it for protection against water damage.

The stream soon became waist high. It was cooler than he expected. The flow was fast, and he had to push against the current. As he moved forward, the tunnel narrowed. Soon it was barely wide enough for a man to pass through. The roof was low and he had to crouch. The cool water sloshed against his chest as he waded further into the darkness.

A hundred feet. Two-hundred feet. Five-hundred. Soon he couldn't get a radio signal. Eventually, even with the night vision goggles, he soon couldn't see anything. There was no light to amplify. The world of illuminated green light he saw through the lenses faded into blackness.

He felt his other senses come into play. The bubbling, flowing water grew louder. The air held a damp, fresh taste to it. The blood thundered in his temples and the hairs on his neck rose high. Every instinct he had screamed danger... Death awaited him at the end of this tunnel.

Despite the tricks his mind was playing on him, Caine kept advancing. He estimated he had travelled over a mile. At one point, something long and slimly slipped past his legs. He assumed it was a snake, but he didn't stop advancing. Then the sensation was gone. Whatever it was, it disappeared into the dark water.

He was starting to think entering the tunnel had been a mistake. But Khaldun had come the same way. The older man did not have much of a head start on Caine, and wasn't nearly as fit. Caine knew he had to keep going; the old man had to be down here.

A few minutes later, he heard voices echoing off the rocks. Men whispering. Low, hushed conversations in Arabic. Then he saw light. Dim and flickering, like a candle in the shadows.

Caine ducked low in the water and advanced. He held his M4 up over his head to keep it dry and battle ready.

Finally, the cramped tunnel opened into a cave. Caine counted three men on a ledge. Two young soldiers, dressed like the insurgents, held Russian AK-47s at their sides. The third man was Khaldun. The honeycomb mass of scarring that disfigured one side of his face seemed to glow red in the candlelight.

Assessing the situation, Caine noticed the water channel disappeared again into the far side of the rock. This place looked to be some kind of storage area. But storing what? Caine was not close enough to see.

Hidden in the water, and in the shadow of the tunnel, Caine aimed his rifle. He squeezed the trigger, quickly putting two bullets into the heads of the two Al Qaeda soldiers. They were dead before they heard the sound of his shots. Before Khaldun could even move, Caine pivoted and fired again. He shot Khaldun twice, once in each calf.

The maimed bomb maker fell to the ground, howling in pain.

Caine listened for other soldiers who might have been out of visual range, but he heard nothing. No one came to Khaldun's aid. Caine advanced, sweeping his rifle across every nook and cranny of the dark cavern. Then he climbed out of the channel, and stood over his fallen enemy.

The Al Qaeda commander spat at Caine. His gnarled hand drew

his Janbiya knife, an ornate blade forged with a rhinoceros horn grip. Khaldun cursed and swung the steel blade, but Caine stood just out of range.

Caine sighed. He slung his rifle over his shoulder. With a single, fluid motion, he drew his M45 pistol and put a bullet through the terrorist's hand. The man screamed again. The knife fell away with a clang, then dropped into the water.

Caine checked the cave. No one else was coming. It was just the two of them.

"Where are the children?" he demanded. His Arabic wasn't as good as Kimberly's, but it was enough.

Khaldun cursed him, his eyes wide and manic.

Caine ignored him. He looked up as voices rose in the darkness. Many distant, tiny voices. Young children, calling out in Arabic for help.

"Never mind." Caine put two bullets in Khaldun's chest, and one in the head. The terrorist's body twitched for a few seconds, as blood gushed from the wounds. Then he froze, and lay lifeless on the cold, wet rocks.

Caine listened again for the calls. What he had thought was a shadowy wall was actually a passage carved into the rock. He picked up a candle and advanced. Soon he came across a cavern, blocked with a wooden door. He forced it open. Dozens of tiny bodies poured forward. Young boys... the children.

He had found them.

They didn't wait for instructions. They jumped into the water and disappeared downstream.

"Mohammad Naaji?" Caine called out to each boy as they passed. "Hussein Naaji?" Most shook their head and kept moving. One did stop, barely eight-years-old, and looked up at Caine. He was dirty and thin, but most of all he was terrified.

"I'm Hussein?" his trembling voice said in Arabic.

"I'm with your mother, Safiya."

"My mother is here?"

Caine nodded. "Yes, I'm going to take you to her. Pass the word down the line. When we get outside, wait at the cave entrance. Don't enter the camp until I give the word. My soldier friend and I are going to cause a distraction. Explosives, like fireworks. You all have to get into the trucks, okay? Then we're going to drive you back to your families."

"You are American?" came a second, older voice.

Caine turned and laid eyes on what was clearly Hussein's older brother, Mohammad. He saw their mother's eyes staring back at him. Their faces held the same hurt and fear she had carried the whole time he had known her.

"Yes. I'm with the U.S. Government. This is a rescue mission."

Mohammad nodded. "Okay. We will pass the word on."

"Thank you. Now let's move!"

Caine waited until the last boy waded down the channel. He counted thirty-seven bodies passing before him. He followed them in the cool water.

As soon as he had a signal, Caine radioed ahead.

"Sergeant Tyler, I have the children and the data stick. We're making our way to the exit, over."

Tyler's voice crackled back. "Roger that. I already thinned the herd a bit out here. Some wandering sentries. Amazing what a man can accomplish with twelve inches of high quality steel. Standing by for your signal."

Caine grinned in the darkness.

The mass of children huddled near the tunnel's exit. Caine jogged up and peered through the opening. He saw the camp fire, still crackling in the distance. Only about half as many men gathered around it as before.

Tyler had been busy.

Caine reloaded his weapons, then turned to the children. "Okay, no one moves until I say. Understood?"

Mohammad and Hussein nodded. The boys whispered instructions amongst themselves.

Caine lifted the radio to his lips. "Tyler... light it up."

"On it..." the voice answered back.

BOOM!

The rocks shook, and dust filled the air. A series of explosions erupted around the edges of the camp. The fireballs were almost blinding in the dim light.

A few of the terrorists who sat near the outskirts of the camp were consumed by the explosions. Their charred bodies flew through the air. The remaining men leapt to their feet, firing their weapons wildly into the darkness.

Tyler's silenced shots dropped men left and right. He was cutting a path through the confused, leaderless soldiers.

A path for Caine and the boys.

Caine fired twice, taking out the men closest to the tunnel.

"Move!" he shouted.

He charged forward, and the boys followed behind him. Caine pivoted left and right, spraying fire on the few men that remained. Many of the terrorists had fled into the rocks. They were young foot soldiers, inexperienced and lacking confidence without a leader. Without Khaldun spurring them on, their resistance was feeble at best.

Caine and Tyler ran the children to the two cattle trucks. He counted them again. Still thirty-seven. "You two," he said to Mohammad and Hussein. "Sit up in the front with me, okay?"

Caine and the two boys piled into the front seat of the truck. More children leapt into the back. He started up the engine and the vehicle rumbled to life. They raced out of the camp, kicking up a cloud of dust in their wake. Caine took the lead, with Tyler and the other children in the truck behind.

They turned a bend to find Safiya Naaji waiting in the road. She stood in the glare of the headlights, staring at the truck with trepidation and hope.

Caine swung open the door. "You'd better get in... I have two boys up here who've been waiting to see you."

When she laid eyes upon Mohammad and Hussein, her face lit up.

Caine realized it was the first time he had seen her smile.

CHAPTER TWENTY-SIX

CAMP LEMONNIER, DJIBOUTI

Kimberley Hustwait's surgery lasted four hours. She had lost a lot of blood, and at one point her heart had stopped beating for ten seconds. But in the end, she pulled through.

Afterwards, still in his bloody scrubs, the surgeon had explained to Caine that Kimberley had been extremely lucky. The knife wound had only nicked her major organs and she had suffered no serious damage. But considering the amount of blood she had lost, they had only just got her to the base in time.

Caine sat with Kimberley in the post anesthetic ward while she slept. He visited her again the next day in the general ward. She was still asleep. He watched the IV fluids drip down one splash at a time through the tube attached to her arm.

It was late into the afternoon when her eyelids flicked open. She glanced around, taking in her surroundings. They were in a drab military hospital ward. Everything was khaki and utilitarian.

"I'm not dead?" she said with surprise.

"You're not dead," Caine said, and laughed. He sat close to her, patting her arm affectionately. "You're on the base in Djibouti. You made it."

She smiled, and Caine saw again how pretty she was. If he wasn't involved in a complex relationship with Rebecca, he knew he would have returned her kiss in the desert.

"The bastard stabbed me," Kimberley said through a grimace of discomfort. "Why the hell did he stab me?"

Caine shrugged. "Well, he's dead now."

Her face twisted with concern. "What about Safiya? And her boys, Mohammad and Hussein?"

"They're fine. They're reunited again. And so are the other children and their families."

His voice softened. "I couldn't have done it without you."

She laughed, then coughed and winced in pain. "Don't make me laugh, Tom. This bloody hurts."

He smiled and just looked at her for a while. He'd been worried that she wouldn't make it. That the time taken to divert the flight to the Al Qaeda camp might have made the difference between life and death for her. This time, he'd gotten lucky. But as the surgeon said, it had been a close call.

"I thought Australians were supposed to be tough?"

"It's a myth we Aussies are happy to encourage. You ever been to Australia, Tom?"

"I've been to Sydney Airport."

She made a scoffing noise. "That's like your favorite band playing at the Big Day Out, and you only buy their souvenir t-shirt."

"Big Day Out?"

"You've never heard of Big Day Out? It's one of our biggest music festivals. You should really visit, Tom."

He nodded. "I think I might."

Kimberley lay back, exhausted. She was joking around, but Caine could see she was still in pain from her injuries. She looked weak and frail, but who wouldn't after such a grievous wound? But he could also see determination in her beautiful blue eyes... She would get through this.

"Why are you looking at me like that?"

"Like what?"

"You look sad, Tom."

He nodded. He knew why. Kimberley was a civilian. He was a covert paramilitary officer with the Central Intelligence Agency. They were two very different kinds of people who didn't mix well in the real world.

It was time to say goodbye.

"You're going to walk out of here soon, aren't you Tom, and I'm never going to see you again?"

He shrugged and held her hand. "Not just yet. And who knows, Kimberley. Anything is possible in this world."

CHAPTER TWENTY-SEVEN

Rebecca Freeling waited for Caine inside Camp Lemonnier's Task Force Compound. The building was home away from home for the Navy SEAL, Army Force Delta and other Special Forces teams that operated behind enemy lines. Yemen was only a hundred miles by boat across the Red Sea, so Djibouti was an ideal location to support their covert missions. It also acted as a logistics hub for drone surveillance, to keep the massive U.S. Military machine operational in this part of the world.

Everyone in the Camp wore either military gear, or was dressed in practical clothing. Like the desert boots, jeans and blue cotton shirt that Caine wore. Dust from the Sahara covered the tables and chairs in the sparse meeting room. Everything was covered in a dull film of grime. Caine had come to associate that stain with military bases across the globe.

But Rebecca looked like the harsh environment around her couldn't touch her. She was stunning in a two-piece navy suit, polished flat shoes and a cream blouse. Her fiery red hair was tied back in a ponytail, and she looked sleek and well groomed. She seemed more like the host of a media event than the tough CIA Case Officer Caine knew her to be.

When she laid eyes on Caine, she shook her head. "What happened to you?"

He knew he was a nasty sight. Bruising and cuts covered his face and hands. A bandage wrapped around his shoulder, showing through beneath his shirt collar, and he wore a brace over his injured knee.

"Oh, you know how it goes," he said, and grinned. "Didn't like what someone said to me, so we had words."

"Words?" She stepped close to him, and parted her lips. She was used to him taking a beating in the field. She had given up worrying about what she considered to be minor injuries.

He wanted to kiss her, but he knew someone could walk in at any moment. They'd agreed to keep their on-again-off-again relationship on the down low. Despite their caution, many of their CIA colleagues had guessed what they were up to. He smiled at her instead.

"You created quiet an incident with the Saudi Government," she said in a low voice.

"I'm sure you've sorted it out."

She smiled and looked over his shoulder, checking if anyone was watching them. "Yes, well, the data you recovered contained some very embarrassing information. Intel that the Saudis want to keep quiet. They won't talk about a U.S. encounter against their military on their sovereign territory, if we promise not to release the details on the stick."

"What was on it exactly?" He caught her eye. "Presuming I have clearance to know?"

"You've already figured out most of it. Martin Delbridge was running an operation smuggling medical supplies out of Yemen. He was working with Colonel Rashid of Saudi Military Intelligence. They made it appear to be the Houthis' doing. Emily Argyle, Jarod Forster and his pilot Charles Li were his on the ground team—"

"But Delbridge was using the Mustang Sally program," Caine

interrupted. He convinced Rashid that he was Forster, so if it all went wrong, Forster would take the fall."

Rebecca nodded. "That's right. When Forster found out, he started gathering evidence of Rashid's and Delbridge's dealings. He even had recordings of Rashid and Delbridge communicating on sat phone. Insurance against Delbridge if he ever tried to set them up."

"So he kills Forster instead." Caine gritted his teeth for a second, then continued. "After that, he eliminated Emily and Li. They were all loose ends."

Rebecca nodded. "Technically, the whole operation was sanctioned high up by our own government. Selling the medicines for a profit... that was his own idea. In the eyes of the CIA, Delbridge may be a criminal, but he isn't a traitor."

"But he still ran?"

Rebecca brushed a strand of hair from her face. "He ran because of you."

"He set me up. Sent me, Kimberley and Safiya into the desert to die. He caused a lot of people to suffer." Caine looked again to Rebecca, but she said nothing. "I presume the pharmaceuticals are now making their way to the UNHCR?"

"Yes, we're dealing with a Frenchman, Jean Marchand. It's all being sorted."

"What's going to happen to Safiya and her boys? I can't imagine Yemen will be a safe place for them for much longer."

"Some good news there, Tom. The United States Government has offered them immigration visas and they've accepted. They should be in California before the end of the month."

Caine nodded. "That still leaves a decision to be made about Martin Delbridge."

"Well this is an interesting situation..."

"How so?"

"Some of the top brass think Delbridge is a hero, that SAND-FIRE was a success. They figure he'll report in eventually. When he does, they'll read him the riot act, of course. But after that he'll be back in the field, sorting out terrorists in another war-torn country. Probably with a big promotion."

"Right," Caine snarled, not hiding his disappointment.

"But there are others who think he's a liability. They believe he'll go too far one day, and compromise national security. Maybe he already has."

"Really? So there's a rift at the Company?"

Rebecca nodded. "Delbridge was selling the Yemen medicine for a profit in Dubai. That was never part of the plan. And Forster's information brought more of his illegal activities to light. He's been shipping conflict diamonds out of the Congo, cocaine out of Colombia. Plus, he earmarked millions of dollars for bogus operations. We're fairly certain he's been pocketing much of that over the years."

"Forster was IT-savvy, so I guess he knew how to follow the money."

She nodded, and they were silent for a moment. Ideas formulated in Caine's mind.

"Delbridge is a bad operator," he said.

"A very bad one."

Caine looked away. He knew what he wanted to do. He also knew he wasn't likely to get permission to do it. Not officially, anyway.

"Where is Delbridge now?" he asked.

"Nobody knows. He's worked in so many countries he could have contacts anywhere in the world. This guy is meticulous... you can bet he had multiple contingencies in place, in case he ever had to run."

"What about Australia?"

Rebecca looked puzzled. "What do you know that I don't?"

Caine remembered back to the snowfields in New Zealand where Emily Argyle had bled to death. She didn't deserve to die like that. Jarod Forster didn't deserve to die of grievous wounds in the bone-dry desert. Three-dozen children didn't deserve to suffer at the hands of fanatical terrorists. Hundreds, if not thousands, didn't deserve to die because the medicines they required to live had been sold for a profit.

All this misery started with Delbridge. Caine was determined it would end with him too.

"I couldn't work out why Emily ran to Australia. She had never been in the country before. But what if she wasn't running? Maybe she was hunting. Forster and Emily must have figured that Delbridge's escape route was into Australia. She went there to expose him. I'll bet anything that's where he is."

Rebecca touched his hand. She was standing so close he could feel her breath upon his neck. Then she whispered, "You've got ten days recovery leave, right?"

Caine grinned.

"I can get you on a military flight to RAAF Base Darwin, with a cover identity as a Marine lieutenant. From there, you would be on your own. You would have until your leave is up, or until Delbridge contacts us and he comes in. Tom, you can't leave any evidence you were ever there."

Caine moved in close, his fingers wrapping around hers, holding her tight. To hell with whatever anyone else might think about their relationship. "You trust me with this?"

"I know you Tom. You're reckless. Sometimes... Sometimes I think you have a death wish. But..."

"But... " He kissed her gently on the ear.

"But, you know what's right and what's wrong. And you always do something about it."

CHAPTER TWENTY-EIGHT

BLUE MOUNTAINS, NEW SOUTH WALES, AUSTRALIA

Caine turned off the main highway, two hours west of Sydney. He followed the dirt track deeper into the bushlands of the Blue Mountains. The landscape was vast eucalyptus forests, dramatic cliffs, natural waterfalls and deep gorges. A misty rain gave the landscape a prehistoric ambience. Instead of dinosaurs, a mob of grey kangaroos hopped across the road in front of him.

One caught its leg on something and Caine noticed a CCTV camera spin around, hidden in the bush. He stopped, got out, and saw a tripwire stretched across the road. It only took a few minutes to reset the camera, and make it loop the last five minutes it had recorded. Then he drove again.

When his black Jeep reached the end of the bush-lined drive, he discovered a large ranch style house built on the edge of a high plateau. An outdoor swimming pool shimmered nearby. Despite the light rain, the views over the cliff edge were spectacular. The Australian bushland stretched before him, filling the horizon.

Caine drove the Jeep back out of sight. He parked it, then ran his hand across his recently cropped hair and shaved beard. He slipped on a pair of leather gloves, then drew his SIG Sauer P226 pistol. The slide clicked as he pulled it back, chambering the first 9mm round. He touched his arm to ensure his fighting knife was strapped in place. Then he walked down the remainder of the drive until he reached the front door.

He stood for a moment, listening. He could hear Joaquin Rodrigo's guitar concerto, Concierto de Aranjuez, playing on a stereo system. The smell of sizzling steak filled the air.

Checking that there were no tripwires or cameras, Caine quietly picked the lock. Then, with his pistol ready, he opened the door and slipped inside. There was another tripwire, strung across the hall. He stepped over it carefully.

He found Martin Delbridge quickly enough. He was in the kitchen, carving his medium rare steak and placing it slice by slice on a white marble plate. He had prepared quite a feast for himself... Caine saw a balsamic vinegar salad, baked potatoes, and a glass full of red wine on the counter.

The kitchen area was connected to a spacious lounge. Leather sofas and a huge flat-screen television dominated the room. What looked to be expensive Aboriginal dot murals hung from the walls. Floor to ceiling windows afforded a view of the magnificent landscape Caine had seen earlier. This was a home that only the ultra-wealthy could afford.

Caine raised his pistol and pointed it at Delbridge's head. He stepped out into the kitchen, his footsteps echoing off the tile floor.

"Fuck!" the CIA man swore as he dropped his steak on the ground, shocked at seeing Caine for the first time.

"You were expecting a call ahead?" Caine asked, his voice low and cold.

"Yes, I fucking was," Delbridge moaned. He looked down at the steak, carving knife still in his hand. "You've ruined my lunch. Thirty Australian dollars you cost me."

"I'm sure you can afford it." Caine made a motion with his pistol. "Drop the knife. Now!"

His opponent relinquished it, impaling the blade in the chopping board.

"Step into the middle of the room, where I can see you," Caine growled. "Do it slow. No sudden movements."

Delbridge's lips curled in a sly grin. "It doesn't have to be like this, Mr. Thomas Caine. Don't forget, I know all about you. You're not as clean as you think. There is so much dirt I could reveal about you. You have no idea who's been pulling your strings... the innocent blood on your hands."

Caine ignored his rambling. "Empty your pockets. Again, do it slowly."

Delbridge did what he was told, careful not to make any sudden movements. He never broke eye contact with Caine. "I made the call you know," he said. "All has been forgiven. I'm coming in. Hell, is that why you're here? Did you come to collect me?"

Caine said nothing.

"Oh, that's not it, is it? You came to kill me." His anger seemed to explode from nowhere. "Well, that's fucking grand isn't it? Seven days! Seven fucking days is all I got to enjoy this place. This was where I was going to retire, Caine. But I don't get that, now, do I?"

Caine examined the room while Delbridge blustered. He was looking for anything his opponent might try to use as a weapon against him. He saw nothing within easy reach, except for a glass aquarium with grass, leaves and dead sticks inside. Delbridge probably had a pet lizard or frog in there. Or possibly a concealed weapon of some kind. Delbridge took a step towards the glass tank.

"You know, Caine, one day you might have to run. Then you'll know what it feels like to be hunted like an animal. I just hope when you do, you learn to cover your tracks better than I did."

Caine's glare intensified. He felt his personality become cold. He was preparing himself to kill. His target was standing right in front of him, lined up in the sights of his gun. And yet he hesitated...

He remembered the people he had seen by the gas station... their emasculated bodies, the stench of death lingering over them.

Delbridge grinned. "Something got to you in Yemen, didn't it, Caine? Made you question what kind of man you are?"

Caine's mind immediately went to the kidnapped children, their terrified eyes as they fled from the Taliban camp.

"Do you know how many people you hurt, Delbridge?" he snarled. "How many died? Just so you could live out your days of luxury, surrounded by all of this?"

Delbridge sighed. Caine tensed as the man walked to the glass cabinet and tapped the glass. There must be some kind of animal in there he was tormenting.

"Don't give me that sanctimonious bullshit, Caine. This is just a game. Sometimes you're the king, like me, and sometimes you're just a pawn, like you. The primary objective of a pawn is to be sacrificed so you can win the game in the end."

Caine lined Delbridge up in his sights. He knew he should just shoot him... but again, he hesitated.

What are you waiting for? his mind screamed. But he still did not pull the trigger.

Delbridge looked back at him. His grin grew even more manic. "Oh, now I see... You want to understand, don't you? You want to know why I did it? Fuck, Caine. You've got to get over yourself." He peered into the aquarium. "You think the pets I have here question why they kill their prey? Of course they don't. There is no reason, not one that you can understand. I just wanted money. It's that simple."

The hairs on the back of Caine's neck began to rise. The pulse in his head beat faster and louder.

"Want to know what I keep in here?" he asked, tapping the glass on the aquarium again. "*Hadronyche versuta*. Funnel fucking web spiders, that's what. I thought this ranch would be the perfect home, but these disgusting hairy black spiders seem to like it here too. I've caught eight in the last few days."

Caine remembered how Delbridge had caressed the scorpion in Sana'a. The man had an unnatural obsession with deadly insects.

"Nasty buggers, Caine. You get bitten by one of these, you'll be dead in fifteen minutes." He moved his hand and pointed to a large spider tapping its forelegs on the glass.

Caine could see it now, fat and black and hairy, with fangs the size of fork prongs.

"Imagine getting bitten by eight."

Caine immediately knew something wasn't right but he reacted too slowly. Delbridge ducked and ran. Caine fired, but his shot missed, and ricocheted off the wall. His aim was thrown off as the aquarium suddenly exploded.

The tank shattered into a thousand pieces, filling the room with flying shards of glass. Caine covered his eyes instinctively, as he felt tiny fragments cut across his skin.

It was a distraction, but that was all Delbridge needed to flee outside.

Caine opened his eyes and stepped forward. He froze in his tracks, as he encountered angry spiders on the floor everywhere. There were a lot more than eight. Black and hairy, each one was about the size of a small child's fist. The horde of arachnids scurried towards him. They reared up and slashed the air, droplets of venom glistening on their dagger-like fangs.

Caine was shocked at their speed and aggressiveness. A mass of the large creatures ran towards his feet.

He tried to stomp them with his boot. He got one, but the others were too quick.

Spotting a tall vase next to the kitchen table, he knocked it to the floor, shattering it around them. One spider was crushed in the impact. The others scattered away from the broken glass.

Caine sprinted outside, gun still in hand, and searched for Delbridge. There was a lot of open space before the tree lines of the bush country. Too far for Delbridge to have run in such a short space of time.

As he passed by the pool a metal projectile rushed past his head. He touched his cheek, realizing it bled from a deep cut. A spear from a spear gun wobbled in the wooden veranda behind him.

He looked into the pool.

Delbridge was lying on the bottom, at least ten feet down. The man was breathing through a scuba tank. Caine had been warned; Delbridge planned everything. Including how he would take on intruders if they entered his property.

His spear gun already reloaded, he fired again.

Caine ducked back just in time. The razor sharp projectile whizzed past his chest, and clanged off a statue near the edge of the pool.

Caine knew that bullets wouldn't travel far enough in water to be lethal at that depth. He sucked in a deep lungful of breath. Then he dove into the pool, swimming down with powerful strokes of his arms and legs. He swam closer to Delbridge, as the man frantically reloaded his weapon.

When Caine was within reach, he pulled the knife from the sheath in his arm.

Delbridge was reloading, preparing another spear.

Caine was upon him. He ripped the mask from Delbridge's face. The man dropped the speargun as the water flooded his eyes and nose. Before he could recover, Caine impaled the knife into the man's gut. Delbridge opened his mouth to scream. Instead his throat exploded with bubbles.

Caine slashed the blade across the man's throat. Delbridge struggled to surface, but Caine held him down until the man became lifeless. His still body was soon obscured by a growing cloud of his own blood.

Caine swam away, pulled himself out of the pool and sat for a moment, panting hard for breath. Concierto de Aranjuez still played on a stereo system back in the house. The funnel web spiders were probably hiding in Delbridge's dirty laundry and linen cupboards by now. He'd have to burn down the property before he left. His blood was all over the floor, linking him to a crime scene.

He heard a phone ringing.

Dripping wet, he walked to a sun chair, were a smart phone chirped and vibrated. The international number on display was from Caine's home country, the United States.

"Too late," Caine said to no one when the unanswered phone call ended. "The bastard is dead now."

He tossed the phone into the pool, and watched it sink, disappearing into the crimson water.

THANK YOU!

Thank you for reading *Sandfire*. If you enjoyed this novella, would you please consider leaving an honest review for it at Amazon? Reviews are critical for helping independent authors bring their books to the attention of readers who might enjoy them. I would truly appreciate it, and it can be as short as you like.

If you would like to learn more about me and my books, please visit my website, andrewwarrenbooks.com, or my Facebook page.

Thank you very much.

AAW

WHAT TO READ NEXT

Thank you for reading *Sandfire*. If you enjoyed this novella, here are some other books featuring betrayed assassin Thomas Caine...

CAINE: RAPID FIRE NOVELLAS

DEVIL'S DUE
A Thomas Caine Novella

COLD KILL
A Thomas Caine Novella

SANDFIRE
A Thomas Caine Novella

THOMAS CAINE NOVELS

TOKYO BLACK
A Thomas Caine Thriller

RED PHOENIX
A Thomas Caine Thriller

FIRE AND FORGET
A Thomas Caine Thriller

ALSO BY AIDEN L. BAILEY

BLOOD IVORY

A Simon Ashcroft Novella

THE ASSYRIAN CONTRABAND

A Simon Ashcroft Novella

THE BENEVOLENT DECEPTION

A Simon Ashcroft Thriller

THOMAS CAINE
will
RETURN!

Please Join my Readers Group!

You might get a chance to read the next Thomas Caine thriller for free! You'll also get access to special sales, contests, and new release info...

Please visit
AndrewWarrenbooks.com
for more details.
Thank you.

ANDREW WARREN

Andrew Warren was born in New Jersey, and studied film, English, and psychology at the University of Miami. He has over a decade of experience in the television and motion picture industry, where he has worked as a post production supervisor, story producer, and writer. He currently lives in Southern California.

Andrew loves to hear from his readers! Please feel free to contact him here:

www.andrewwarrenbooks.com
andrew@andrewwarrenbooks.com

AIDEN L. BAILEY

Formerly an engineer, Aiden L Bailey built a career marketing multinational technology, heavy industry and construction companies. His various roles have included corporate communications with the Australian Submarine Corporation, technical writing for several defense contractors, engineering on a petroleum pipeline constructed in the Australian desert, and a magazine editor and art director. He travelled widely in his twenties, predominately through Australia, Africa, Europe and South America, and returned home with many stories to tell. Aiden lives with his wife and daughter in South Australia.

To learn more, visit Aiden's website at aidenlbailey.com

Join Aiden's Readers Group and and receive a FREE Thriller. To join, visit aidenlbailey.com.

Printed in Great Britain
by Amazon

63021806R00112